Across the Rio Grande

When Matt and his cousin Luke, a notorious bounty hunter, are besieged by the Mexicalaros, they know that they must fight their way to victory or die trying.

Everyone knows the Mexicalaros: the renegade gang who terrorize ranches and settlements on both sides of the Rio Grande are feared by all. Now, the cousins are forced to use that fear to recruit help from both sides of the border and to lead a counter-attack on the deadly Mexicalaros.

But will the Mexicalaros hit back? And how many must be slain before peace can return to the border? As Matt and Luke hunt for the leader of the deadly gang, the time has come to find out what the cousins are made of. . . .

Across the Rio Grande

Edwin Derek

A Black Horse Western

ROBERT HALE · LONDON

© Edwin Derek 2010
First published in Great Britain 2010

ISBN 978-0-7090-8984-1

Robert Hale Limited
Clerkenwell House
Clerkenwell Green
London EC1R 0HT

www.halebooks.com

Typeset by
Derek Doyle & Associates, Shaw Heath
Printed and bound in Great Britain by
CPI Antony Rowe, Chippenham and Eastbourne

CHAPTER ONE

The bullet smashed into the boulder a few paces to his left and ricocheted harmlessly away. Until that moment, another day of hard riding had revealed nothing new. And yet, another hundred head of JT cattle had been rustled. Then, as if by magic, had disappeared.

Matt spurred Lucky into action. The mustang responded by breaking into a zigzagging gallop, normally reserved for cutting-out steers. Two more shots rang out but neither came close. They came from somewhere on the hill behind him. But were they warning shots or were the snipers unable to get a bead on Matt due to Lucky's unpredictable course?

Either way, Matt wasn't going to stay to find out. It took time to reload a Springfield, or any of its

Confederate equivalents, so using that time, he intended to get well out of range. And he succeeded; at least, no further shots were fired at him. Nevertheless, he kept Lucky at full gallop, not reining in the mustang until they were well clear. Only then, did he pause to check to see if they were being followed. They weren't; the trail behind them was as deserted as the one ahead.

The lack of pursuers suggested to Matt that his assailants were neither the Kiowa-Apaches nor their Apache cousins. The latter normally lived on the Mexican side of the Rio Grande, but had often crossed the mighty river to raid deep into Texas.

Looking for an easy coup, a war party from either tribe would have given chase. Therefore, it was not unreasonable to assume that the shots had come from the rustlers. In which case, Matt might be close to picking up the trail of the JT ranch's missing cattle.

His hunch proved to be correct. It wasn't long before he picked up the tracks of a herd roughly the size of the one missing from the JT ranch. He followed them until they joined up with another larger herd.

However, where the tracks merged, the grass had been well cropped. There was also a considerable amount of sun-baked dung, so Matt concluded the larger herd had been waiting for the rustled JT steers. The tracks of the combined herd led to Desolation Ford, the only safe place for cattle to cross the Rio Grande for many miles. But then, why had the rustlers driven the herd into Mexico?

A generation ago, Texas had fought ferociously to gain independence from Mexico. It had been a brutal and bloody war and Mexicans, seeking revenge, had continued to raid across the Rio Grande long after peace had been officially declared. Unfortunately, the Lone Star State's only official defence against these raids had been a handful of Rangers.

Yet, after only a few years of independence, Texas had opted to join the United States. At that time, the Rio Grande had been officially ratified by treaty as the border between the United States and Mexico. As a result, the cavalries of both nations had been forbidden by their respective govern-ments to cross the Rio Grande. It was an edict observed scrupulously by both sides.

However, the formerly independent Texas had used slave labour, especially on its cotton plantations. Its adoption into the already divided United States was undoubtedly one of the catalysts to the start of the Civil War. Since the end of those hostilities, the Rangers, unarguably sympathetic to the Confederate cause, had been disbanded by the new Yankee taskmasters of Texas.

Their replacement, the State Police, had been mainly recruited from Yankee, city based, police institutions. They had little experience of Indian fighting or patrolling the vast untamed expanses of the Texas panhandle, so border patrols were infrequent and ineffectual. As a result, raids on border ranches went largely unchecked even in the larger and supposedly more civilized part of Texas, east of the Pecos river.

The Pecos river flowed southwards through Texas and into the Rio Grande. If the patrols of the State Police were infrequent in the eastern half of Texas, they were non-existent west of the Pecos. To make matters worse, the newly formed United States Cavalry were, as yet, too few in number to make any real impact.

So the vast wilderness west of the Pecos had become a haven for hostile Indians, outlaws, rustlers, whiskey peddlers – to the Indians – and, worst of all, gun-runners. Indeed, the only law west of the Pecos was that of the six-gun. And west of the Pecos was where Matt now lived.

But it was across the mighty Rio Grande the cattle had been driven and so were lost forever.

The hills on the Mexican side of the great river were reputedly the home of the mysterious Mexicalaros whose reputation was even more fearsome than the Apaches.

Indeed, although it was rumoured that there were several Americans in the Mexicalaros, they had not hesitated to scalp anyone foolhardy enough to cross the Rio Grande and enter what they considered to be their territory. Yet, these rustlers had done just that. So did that mean they were Mexicalaros? Matt hoped not, for they numbered at least fifty and, even if they were split into separate gangs as he believed, even one gang would be too many for the JT ranch to handle.

Night was rapidly approaching, making further investigation impossible. Indeed, day time patrolling in this part of the border was considered dangerous by the newly formed US Cavalry and they did not patrol during the hours of darkness.

However, this was not because of any possible danger. Quite the opposite. Many of the US Cavalry's West Point trained officers considered the Indians to be superstitious savages afraid to fight at night. They believed Indians would not fight at night for fear that their spirits could not then find their way to the Happy Hunting Grounds should they be killed during the hours of darkness.

9

In Texas, at least, nothing could have been further from the truth. Using the stars to guide them, it was not unknown for the Kiowa-Apache to raid ranches and even quite large settlements under the cover of darkness. Unfortunately, the Cavalry often attributed these raids to Mexican bandits.

As daylight began to turn to dusk, Matt thought he detected movement in front of him. But by the time he reached the spot, it was deserted. Nor were there any signs of anybody having been there.

'Guess I'm getting a mite jumpy,' he muttered ruefully to his horse who neighed as if in agreement.

It was now too late to return to the JT ranch house, so Matt decided to head for the nearest line cabin. Even by Texas standards, the JT was a large ranch, but unfortunately, in its case, size had not brought wealth. Nevertheless, it had several well stocked line cabins on the edges of its vast territory.

The particular line cabin Matt headed towards was unique. Originally, it had been part of a much larger stockade containing several adobe buildings. They had been built by the Mexicans long before the war against Texas.

However, before they had been driven out, the

Mexicans had destroyed most of the stockade leaving only one building and a corral standing. Still far larger and more substantial than a typical line cabin, it had become an outpost for the Rangers.

After the Rangers had been disbanded, the JT ranch had taken over this adobe building and used it as a base for its cowboys tending cattle on that part of its range. But now, times were hard. Apart from Matt and a few older hands left to look after the ranch, the rest were driving the JT herd east across Texas until they reached the Chisholm trail. Then, they would follow it northwards for many a weary week until they eventually reached a newly developed railhead town called Dodge.

So, Matt expected the line cabin to be unoccupied. But it was not – smoke coming out of its chimney indicated someone had taken up residence. Could it be one or more of the rustlers?

As Matt neared the cabin, he saw a superb black stallion hitched outside it. It was the finest looking horse he had ever seen. But where was its owner? He was about to find out.

Matt dismounted as quietly as he could, yet, as he did so, he heard the ominous sound of a rifle being cocked. The occupant of the line cabin had outsmarted him: whilst Matt's attention had been diverted by the magnificent stallion, his adversary had got the drop on him.

Matt was almost blinded by the setting sun, now almost hidden by the horizon, but he could make out the barrel of an unusual looking rifle pointing directly at his chest.

CHAPTER TWO

Matt cursed openly at his stupidity for walking into such an obvious trap. But, instead of shooting, his unseen adversary burst out into laughter. The laugh was followed by a voice which had a familiar southern accent, perhaps a little more refined than his own.

'Well now, my friend, this is a pleasant surprise. You're a long way from home!'

Matt recognized the voice instantly. Yet he had to be wrong, for it sounded like his cousin, Luke. They had grown up together and had once been the greatest of friends. But, when the Civil War came, his cousin had sided with the Yankees while he had joined the Confederate Army.

Luke had gone on to become one of the Yankees most respected scouts, but that had not stopped the Yankee army, under General Grant, from destroying his family's plantation as they advanced down the Shenandoah Valley.

Possibly, that was why Matt's cousin had only briefly returned at the end of the Civil War. He left after only a few days, leaving the remains of the plantation in the safe hands of Matt's elder brother. As far as Matt knew, Luke had never returned.

In the years that followed, his cousin Luke had become a notorious bounty hunter, building up a fearsome reputation for hunting down outlaws wanted 'dead or alive'. And dead, *had been* his preferred way of returning his quarry to the authorities.

Had been, for Matt's cousin was dead. Surprisingly, he had become the sheriff of the small town called Redrock. In that capacity, he had become embroiled in a range war and been killed.

The sad news travelled slowly but eventually reached Matt at the JT ranch. So he had travelled many miles to visit his cousin's grave in order to pay his last respects.

'Well Matt Connelly, I see you've still not learnt the art of approaching buildings quietly.'

The owner of the voice lowered the barrel of his strange looking rifle and stepped out of the blinding rays of the setting sun. For the first and only time in his life, Matt froze, for indeed, he was looking at the smiling face of his cousin, Luke Donovan, whose grave he had travelled so far to visit, just a few months ago.

Clearly his cousin was still alive. Indeed, his reported death had not prevented him from getting married. The plain gold ring he wore on the third finger of his left hand glinted brightly in the last rays of the dying sun.

'When you've come to your senses, we had better put the horses in the corral and then grab a meal,' said Luke, still grinning broadly. 'I think we have some catching up to do.'

Once inside the adobe line cabin, Matt busied himself by closing its thick wooden shutters and bolting the cabin door. Luke, meanwhile, was busily stirring a cauldron containing jack rabbit stew which bubbled merrily over the now blazing fire. It smelled good, but then Luke had become an expert at living off the land.

'You're looking a might sprightly for a dead man,' said Matt as he helped himself to a bowl of the stew.

'Can't complain,' replied Luke.

'I rode over to Redrock and saw your grave. Not that I am not pleased to see you alive, but how come you're not in it?'

'Because I met a girl called Elizabeth. As a bounty hunter and gunman I couldn't safely settle down especially after her pa, who was the mayor of Redrock, appointed me sheriff.'

'What happened to the original one?' asked Matt.

'He was murdered,' replied Luke.

'Murdered?'

'Yes. My predecessor discovered that a ranch owner called Colonel Masters had advance information about a railroad's intention to run a spur line into Redrock. Masters kept that news to himself and decided to buy up all the land the railroad needed. Of course, he intended to sell the land to the railroad at a huge profit. He made several purchases but then got greedy and hired gunmen to drive off any landowner who wouldn't sell.'

'From my trip to Redrock, I gather he didn't succeed,' said Matt drily.

'No, a few good men, and women too, stood up to him,' replied Luke.

'So what happened to you?' asked Matt.

'There was a lot of shooting and I got hit. But as you see, not as badly as the good folk of Redrock were led to believe.'

'So who is in your grave?' asked Matt.

'Another dead gunman.'

'But Luke, why the deception?'

'As I said, so I could settle down with Elizabeth. I didn't want some young gunslinger, looking to make a reputation, turning up in Redrock and calling me out. Not that I have any fears in drawing against anybody but I have already brought enough violence into Elizabeth's life.'

'But Luke, wouldn't the townsfolk of Redrock have discovered that you were still alive?'

'Of course. Hence my make-believe funeral. Then Elizabeth, accompanied by her mother, went back East to visit relatives. However, they first went to St Louis where I was waiting for them. Mrs Grande supervised the arrangements and Elizabeth and I got married there.'

'Didn't anybody recognize you or at least connect your name to the dead bounty hunter?' asked Matt.

'No, because instead of my bride changing her name to mine, I changed my name to hers. Then, almost immediately after we got married, Elizabeth and her mother actually went to stay with their relatives back East.'

'You didn't go with your new bride?' exclaimed Matt.

17

'No,' said Luke somewhat ruefully. 'I had quite a bit of money put by from my bounty hunting days, so whilst Mrs Grande was busy supervising our marriage arrangements, acting as my agent, Mr Grande bought a ranch in Texas near Butte Springs. It's called Pine Valley. It's further up the Rio Grande, although the Mexicans call their side of it, the Rio Bravo.'

'That's great. As the crow flies, Butte Springs is little more than a hundred miles away. By Texas standards, we're almost neighbours,' exclaimed Matt.

'Perhaps, although it's not like the good old days in Virginia. But I guess those days can never return,' said Luke thinking of his former home.

'I guess not. But you haven't explained what you're doing on the JT ranch, apart from scaring me to death,' said Matt.

'Although the Pine Valley ranch is small by Texas standards, we own about fifteen hundred acres. However, the deal was also supposed to include a herd of branded cattle. We were also assured that there were hundreds of branded steers roaming on our range, ours for the taking. But unfortunately, so far I have not located any and there seems to be only a handful of unbranded ones.'

Matt frowned. That didn't make sense. Whatever other faults they may have had, almost all the Texans he had met had been men of their word. In a land where few could read or write, a handshake on a deal was every bit as good as a legally binding contract. If the deal had included branded cattle, Matt would have bet his life the full amount would have been found somewhere on the ranges of the ranch. But he said nothing.

'I'd almost given up searching for them when I found tracks of a small herd. Although they were a few days old, I decided to follow them,' said Luke.

'And they brought you here?' asked Matt.

'Yes. They led from our range, to the banks of the Rio Grande. But they didn't cross it. Instead, they followed the bank for many miles until they crossed near here.'

'The crossing is called Desolation Ford,' said Matt.

'Judging by the signs, before they were driven across Desolation Ford, my steers were held in wait for another herd to join them.'

'I guess that would be the herd I was trailing. I work for the JT ranch, but times are hard and the ranch is losing more cattle than it can afford,' said Matt grimly.

'Well,' said Luke, 'I reached Desolation Ford

earlier today, but I was too late. The steers had already crossed the Rio Grande. I thought about following them into Mexico, but I could hardly recapture them and then drive them back to Pine Valley by myself. So while I was deciding what to do next, I scouted around and found this cabin.'

'Just as well you didn't follow them. The range of hills on the other side of the Rio Grande is the home of the Mexicalaros. Even the Apache avoid them,' said Matt grimly.

'That bad! I was going to pick up their trail tomorrow. Seems you may have saved my neck.'

'Scalp more like. The Mexicalaros are more deadly than any Indian war party,' said Matt. 'But Luke, it seems like we are on similar errands. As I said, the JT ranch is also missing stock. I'd just picked up their trail when somebody starting shooting at me.'

'It wasn't me, or you would be dead,' laughed Luke. 'I only heard the shooting in the distance. So I rode to see what was happening. When I saw the rider hadn't been hit, I circled round in front of him but returned to the cabin when I saw he wasn't being followed. However, I have to admit that I didn't recognize you. You've grown up some since we last met.'

'The war had a way of doing that to a man,' Matt

replied grimly.

After a long debate, they came to the conclusion that the rustlers were most probably the Mexicalaros. But why they should rustle branded cattle when there were still a countless number of unbranded ones roaming free on the panhandle was a mystery that neither Matt or Luke could explain.

CHAPTER THREE

Early the next morning, Matt awoke to the sound of gunfire. Luke and his unusual looking rifle were both missing, but Josh, Luke's big black stallion was still in the corral.

There was no further shooting, so Matt concluded that Luke had been hunting for breakfast. He was right, for just as coffee was ready, his cousin returned with another brace of jack rabbits. However, the sounds of rapidly approaching horsemen meant there was no time to do anything with them.

Bullets thudded into the white adobe cabin wall, indicating the unfriendly intentions of the unwelcome visitors. However, by that time, Luke and Matt were already inside the line cabin and had bolted its solid oak door.

It seemed that some of the rustlers had backtracked and re-crossed the Rio Grande. No doubt they had been near enough to hear the sound of Luke's rifle and had decided to investigate.

In its time, the old cabin had withstood several prolonged sieges from border raiders. Hitherto, it had proved to be more than a match for its would-be conquerors, but then, there had always been sufficient numbers to defend it.

Although there were ample supplies of food and water, the cabin's size counted against its present day defenders. Apart from front and kitchen doors, its sides had windows, four in total, but there was only Luke and Matt to defend them – not that they were going to surrender without a fight.

Making himself clearly visible to the rustlers, Matt stood by the window close to the front door. A ragged fusillade of shots was directed at him but this time, none came that close. Matt was too experienced to return the fire. Instead, he counted the flashes made by the enemy's rifles.

'I make it eight guns, but they're out of range, so I guess they're only trying to pin us down. How's things at the back?'

'Nothing's happening,' replied Luke staring

23

intently out of the small kitchen window.

But Matt caught sight of some movement by the enemy.

'There soon will be,' he said grimly. 'Two men are beginning to circle round the cabin. I guess they're making for the corral, but even if I could get a clear shot, I think they're out of range.'

But he had to try. Their horses were in the corral. If the raiders got them, Luke and Matt would be stranded. Even if they managed to beat off the rustlers, on foot they would stand little chance of surviving.

So, ignoring the danger of being hit by a lucky shot, Matt leant out of the window. The two rustlers had not reached the corral, but as he suspected, his bullet hit the ground fully ten paces short of the men.

Bullets thudded into the window frame an inch above his head. While he had been concentrating on the two men trying to get to the back of the ranch house, the rest of the rustlers had reloaded and had edged nearer to the line cabin: this time, their shots were in range.

This time, Matt counted nine gun flashes. Including the two circling it and probably one more looking after their horse, Matt reckoned they were facing twelve men.

24

After years at war, Matt could tell the besiegers were using single shot muzzle-loading Springfields or Confederate copies. Expertly, he began to reload, a relatively slow and complex affair. Charge and bullet had to be rammed down its muzzle and then the Springfield still had to be primed before it could be fired again. In spite of years of practice, by the time he had reloaded, the two men circling the line cabin had moved out of sight.

Once they reached the rear of the big line cabin they would be partly protected by the far end of the corral and would keep Matt fully occupied. Then, while he and Luke were pinned down by fire from in front and behind, more gunmen would undoubtedly work their way around to the side of the line cabin and take the horses. Then, the rest of the rustlers would surely turn their attention to the cabin's undefended side windows.

The rest of the rustlers moved backwards, just far enough to be out of range of Matt's Springfield. But two more of them left the main group and, as Matt had anticipated, also began to work their way around the cabin. However, this time, Matt saved his ammunition and did not fire; he had already proved they were out of range. Yet at the back of the kitchen, Luke would soon have four to deal with. The odds seemed to be stacking up against them.

But Matt had underestimated his cousin, or rather, the unusual looking rifle which he was holding. Luke moved swiftly to the side window. Through its slats, he could clearly see the first two gunmen who, believing they were out of range of any musket rifle, stood up and waited for the other two rustlers to join them.

But it worked both ways. If they were out of range of the cabin, Luke was also out of range of their weapons. So he fully opened the shutters and aimed the unusual rifle at the first two gunmen. However, it was not a single shot musket rifle and without reloading, he fired twice in rapid succession. In spite of the distance, both bullets struck their intended targets and both rustlers crashed to the ground, never to move again.

Still without reloading, Luke fired at the other two rustlers. But seeing their colleagues fall, they dived to the ground and rolled out of sight. Nevertheless, Luke was pretty sure he had hit one of them.

He then moved quickly to the front window and, still without reloading, continued to fire. The rest of the rustlers, who also thought they were out of range, soon discovered they were not. Shot after shot rang out from Luke's rifle until, at last, it had to be reloaded. But by then, at least three more raiders had been fatally hit.

Even though it came from just one rifle, the fusillade was enough to convince the surviving rustlers the line cabin was too well defended to be taken. They even abandoned their attempt to steal the horses in the corral. Instead, they raced to their own horses and rode away as quickly as they had arrived, leaving their dead but taking the dead men's horses with them.

Matt realized that, in spite of its failure, the raid had been planned with a precision not normally associated with cattle rustlers. It confirmed his suspicions that they were Mexicalaros. Had it not been for Luke's remarkable repeating rifle, the like of which Matt had never before encountered, neither he nor his cousin could have survived.

As soon as they were sure the rustlers were not going to return, Luke and Matt left the cabin to examine the fallen: there were six in all.

Three of the four rustlers who had tried to circle round to the back of the cabin had paid in full for the attempt. Unfortunately, their bodies revealed little of interest, so Matt and Luke moved on to search the bodies at the front of the cabin. The fourth man was of a similar ilk to the first three. One of the other bodies, however, proved to be of greater interest.

Although it was now several years since the end of the Civil War, the dead man was dressed in a remarkably new-looking Confederate officer's uniform. He possessed two brand new fifty dollar pieces and carried papers identifying him as Captain Nathan Masters.

This revelation sent a cold shiver down Luke's back. The man behind their troubles in Redrock had been Colonel Masters. But hadn't he been a Yankee? If so, the names may just have been a coincidence, yet Luke didn't think so.

The dead man also toted an old Griswold & Gunnison six-gun, a weapon only used in the Confederate army. In fact, it was a copy of the Colt Navy 'Old Model' handgun and, like the original, had been fitted with a hexagonal barrel, however, it was easily distinguishable from the vastly superior Colt. Owing to an acute shortage of metal in the south during the latter part of the Civil War, its frame had been made of brass. Perhaps that was why the other rustlers had not taken it with them.

Both Matt and Luke instantly recognized the rifle-musket the dead Confederate captain had been carrying. Made in their home state by the Richmond Armoury of Virginia, it was another Confederate copy of a Union weapon, this time a copy of the Springfield 1861 rifle-musket: the very one that Luke used.

However, although the copy looked fairly similar to the original, its bore was .577 instead of the .580 of the original. This apparently slight difference gave the Confederates an advantage over their Union rivals. The ammunition designed for the Union weapon could not be used in its copy, although the Richmond Army rifle-musket could fire the ammunition of the Springfield original. During the war, literally tens of thousands had been made and today, they could be purchased in many gunsmiths for next to nothing.

Luke gave one of the silver fifty dollar pieces to Matt. It was no good to the dead man so he took it gratefully, especially since it represented a little over seven weeks' pay.

They buried the dead in a shallow communal grave which they marked with a few stones. Although on opposite sides, both Luke and Matt were Civil War veterans, so the grisly task did not put them off their much delayed breakfast. Once they had finished it, they doused the fire, saddled up and set off for the JT ranch: a council of war was required with its owner, Mr Thompson.

CHAPTER FOUR

They rode hard. Matt's unusually large mustang, fine horse though it was, could not match the stamina of Luke's magnificent stallion, Josh.

'He's a pure bred Barb. A long time ago, his ancestors came from the Barbary Coast,' explained Luke when they stopped to rest Matt's mustang.

'So how did they get over here?' asked Matt.

'They were the mounts of the Muslim army during their invasion of Spain over a thousand years ago. The Spanish bred them and centuries later their Conquistadors brought some of them to South America.'

'How did you come by Josh?' asked Matt.

'Spoils of war,' replied Luke, evading a direct answer.

'Tell me about your amazing rifle, I've seen

nothing like it.'

'It's a Henry and it was a present from my father-in-law.'

'That's a new name to me,' said Matt.

'Made by Colt. Like the Spencer, it's a breach-loader, but unlike my old Spencer, it doesn't jam when it gets hot. In fact, the Henry keeps on working no matter how long you keep firing. And, of course, its rate of fire is much faster than the muzzle loading Springfield.'

After much hard riding, they arrived at the JT ranch an hour before sundown. The massive ranch house was almost deserted and Luke thought it had seen better days: evidence of neglect was plain to see.

Although several years had passed since the end of hostilities, the aftermath of the Civil War still managed to cast its long dark shadow across this remote part of Texas, although it had been many miles away from the main hostilities of the War.

John Thompson had owned the ranch for almost twenty years and it was from his initials that it took its name. But neither that nor his forty years had stopped him joining the Confederate army. He had served under General 'Stonewall' Jackson and earned a field commission in spite of his lack of West Point training. Matt had served under him as a master sergeant.

When the Civil War was over, Matt had returned to the Shenandoah Valley to find that his home, in common with many other plantations, was in ruins; only his brother had survived. His parents and most of the people he had grown up with had been killed or moved on.

Matt had no money to help rebuild his old home. In any case, without slaves to work in the fields, he believed the plantation was not viable. His brother had thought otherwise.

Unfortunately, there had been no suitable paid work available for Matt and he would not sponge off his hard working brother, so he had taken up the long standing invitation to work for his former commanding officer on his Texas ranch.

As a former major in the Confederate army, John Thompson was treated with deep suspicion by the new Yankee masters of Texas, especially as the JT ranch had been virtually a second home to the Rangers. There were those now in power who, unfortunately, would neither forgive nor forget the role the ranch had played in supporting the Rangers.

At first, the presence of Mrs Thompson at dinner muted conversation, even though she made the trail-stained Luke feel at home. As the meal progressed, Luke discovered she was both intelligent and perceptive. Indeed, it was she who ran the ranch's finances. Mr Thompson may have done the actual hiring, but his wife decided how many and for how long.

However, the JT ranch was in severe financial difficulty as its owner readily admitted. Most of John Thompson's funds had been in Confederate currency, worthless now Texas banks were under Yankee ownership.

At first, this had not been a problem as the ranch had managed to obtain the credit necessary to keep it running, but the bank had been forced to withdraw that facility by the Yankee carpet-baggers and the ranch's outstanding mortgage had been called in. The JT ranch was surviving on borrowed time and only the sale of its herd, currently heading northwards along the Chisholm Trail, could avert repossession.

The herd had already been on the trail for three months, so it would reach Dodge in the next few weeks; the steers would have to be sold and the trail hands paid. Most of them would then make for the saloons and there they would stay until they had no money left to pay for liquor or the special pleasures provided by the saloon girls. Only then would the cowboys begin the return journey to the

JT ranch and, even without the herd to slow them down, that would take another three to four weeks.

Inevitably, the conversation turned to the morning's shootings and the problem of the missing cattle. Owing to the aforementioned cattle drive, though, none of the few remaining JT ranch hands could be spared to go after the missing cattle.

However, Mr. Thompson agreed that Matt could accompany Luke back to his Pine Valley ranch and use it as a base to track down the rustlers.

'But what can two do against a gang of rustlers?' asked Mrs Thompson.

'Locate their base, so when our men return, we can go after them,' replied Mr Thompson.

'We?' repeated Mrs Thompson.

'I'm not yet so old and decrepit that I can't go after a few pesky rustlers,' replied Mr Thompson. But his voice had a defensive tone.

The next day, as dawn broke, Luke and Matt set out for the Pine Valley ranch. Matt had switched horses and was now mounted on a chestnut stallion called Spike. Unlike Josh, a pure bred Barb, Spike was a horse of many breeds and even more moods, few of which were good. As a result, few JT hands chose to ride him, but it seemed the horse tolerated Matt better than most other riders.

The western perimeter of the huge but debt ridden JT range was over a day's ride from the ranch house. So they spent the night at the ranch's western line cabin. Made from cottonwood, it was a much smaller building than the one in which they had been attacked. This time, however, there were no such interruptions and they left early the next morning.

Luke had been away from Pine Valley for several days and hoped Elizabeth and her mother had arrived during his absence. He missed Elizabeth greatly and hoped his days of roving were now behind him.

They rode steadily through some of the harshest landscape Matt had ever seen; unbranded longhorns browsed contentedly on sagebrush and wire-like grass. Again came the question: why would anybody risk rustling branded cattle, for which the penalty was hanging, when the Panhandle was full of unbranded longhorns?

They reached Pine Valley at sunset. Why the ranch was so called was another mystery: there was a complete absence of pine trees in what was more like a huge crater than a valley, but there was an abundance of water, for a shallow lake filled the centre of the crater.

In spite of his lack of breeding, Spike had

matched his illustrious companion every pace of the way, much to the annoyance of Josh. And Spike's manners had improved: determined to prove his worth, he actually enjoyed the journey and so had given Matt an easier ride than he had expected.

Luke hailed the hacienda style ranch house and was instantly rewarded with a gleeful response. Elizabeth rushed out to greet him: as soon as he dismounted, she flung her arms around him and Luke returned her embrace with interest. So far, since they had been married, they had only been able to spend two nights together.

'I take it this lady is your wife, otherwise you could be in a lot of trouble,' said Matt drily as he dismounted. However, he found further comment was made impossible by the appearance of another young woman.

Except to Matt, she was not just another woman: she was the most beautiful creature he had ever seen. Behind her was a stout, stocky man probably in his mid to late forties. His remarkable curly hair had once been jet black, but now contained several grey strands which matched the colour of his bushy sideburns.

Luke, still very much a southern gentleman, made the introductions. The middle-aged man was his father-in-law, Jeremiah Grande and the other girl was Laura Grande, Elizabeth's cousin.

Although not as large as the JT ranch house, the inside of Pine Valley ranch was really quite big and its staircase was especially grand. A Mexican maid escorted Matt to his bedroom and a little later returned with the news that separate bathtubs had been prepared for the new arrivals.

Most of the house had been lavishly rebuilt by the previous owner, yet the hacienda had an ageless ambience. Indeed, parts of it dated back to the days of the Spanish conquistadors.

Judging by the number of Mexican workers around the place, Matt thought that Luke must have amassed a considerable amount of money during his time as a bounty hunter. Yet, in spite of a cook – Chinese not Mexican – Elizabeth insisted on cooking and serving the main course as she had once done when Luke first stayed at their farm near Redrock. That was before Mr Grande had purchased the ranch which had belonged to Colonel Masters, the man Luke and friends had defeated in the Redrock range war.

The main course consisted of steak – what else in Texas, where millions of longhorns roamed on its Panhandle? – roast potatoes and other various vegetables. It was followed by apple pie topped with fresh cream.

In honour of Luke's return, Mrs Grande cooked the pie, again to the annoyance of the Chinese cook who regarded the kitchen as his own property. Indeed, he resented the presence of anyone else in it, even if they were his employers.

Matt guessed Mrs Grande must be in her early forties. Although she had the odd wisp of grey in her otherwise blonde hair, she was still very good looking. Her daughter, Elizabeth, was also a rare beauty; she had a near perfect figure and pene- trating, cornflower blue eyes. The classical features of her face were perfectly framed by her beautiful long hair which was the colour of sun-ripened corn. Matt thought Luke to be a very lucky man.

Nevertheless, it was her cousin, Laura Grande, who was the focus of Matt's attention. The family resemblance was so strong she could have been Elizabeth's sister, but Laura's equally long hair was chestnut and her eyes were hazel – eyes which seemed to follow Matt's every move, or was that just wishful thinking on his part?

Over dinner, Matt described the incident at the line cabin and the problems the JT ranch were having with rustlers. Laura was eastern bred and unused to the violence of the West, so her face turned ghostly white as Matt described the raid and the killing of the raiders. Elizabeth, however, listened to his story without reacting, even when Mr Grande began to ask questions.

'Enough, Jeremiah,' said Mrs Grande, who had noticed Laura's reaction to the shootings.

Obediently, he changed the subject immediately. When he was in favour, his wife called him Jerry, but whenever he displeased her, it was Jeremiah, a name she knew he hated.

CHAPTER FIVE

Matt overslept, so by the time he awoke the ranch was already a hive of activity. But it was Mrs Grande directing the workforce, not her husband. He had gone out before dawn in the wagon, but the trip was shrouded in mystery. Even Mrs Grande did not know the reason for her husband's sudden departure or where he was going.

A group of Mexicans laboured busily in an attempt to restore the old barn to something like its former glory. Several more appeared to be cleaning out the bunk-house but Mrs Grande was not impressed with their efforts and was busy telling them so as Matt approached her. She would not let him help, insisting he was a guest and in any case, it was time for breakfast. As Laura was just about to start her breakfast, Matt readily agreed.

'I understand you haven't seen your cousin Luke for some years, although you used to be neighbours in Virginia,' said Laura breaking an awkward silence.

'That's right,' said Matt. 'My uncle, Luke's father, inherited one of the biggest plantations in the Shenandoah Valley. Apparently, there had been some long-standing disagreement between my father and the rest of the family so he was left nothing until Luke's father bought the neigh-bouring plantation and gave it to him. They never got on but that didn't stop me playing with Luke when we were little.'

'So what happened?'

'Although my uncle kept slaves, he was an Abolitionist and treated them like paid employees. Luke had just graduated from West Point when the Civil War broke out and joined the Union Army as a Lieutenant. My father was a true southerner, so I enlisted in the Confederate army.'

'Why didn't you meet up again after the war was over?'

'I returned home to find all my family, except my brother, had been killed and both plantations had been burnt to the ground. Luke had returned home but left again before I got back. There was nothing left for me in Virginia so I also moved on.'

41

'How sad, Matt, but what are you going to do now?'

It was the first time Laura had used his name and she made it seem special.

'Help Luke locate the rustlers and then run them off.'

If the Mexicalaros were the rustlers, that wasn't going to be as easy as Matt made it sound. However, the arrival of Elizabeth and Luke, arm in arm, caused a change of subject.

'My bossy wife insists I spend the day with her,' said Luke, grinning broadly, 'so I guess you two have got the day free.'

Having sorted the Mexican labourers, Mrs Grande returned to the dining room in time to hear Luke's comments. They gave her an idea which she was not slow to voice.

'Matt, it's a beautiful day. Jerry won't be back until this evening, so if Luke thinks it's safe, why don't you take Laura for a ride in the buggy? You could take a picnic.'

'Providing you don't go too far away from the ranch house, it should be safe enough, especially if you take my Henry rifle with you,' said Luke.

At first Laura said nothing although she blushed profusely at the suggestion. Matt took her silence to mean that she didn't want to go with him, but was too embarrassed to say so. But he was completely wrong.

Her strict upbringing, rather than her feelings, was the reason for Laura's apparent reticence. Until a few weeks ago, she had lived all her young life back east in Boston but at the insistence of Elizabeth, she had come to the Pine Valley ranch on a extended holiday to learn about life in the West.

Back in Boston, etiquette had been so formalized that it dictated that respectable and well-bred young ladies must be formally introduced before they could acknowledge any young man. Then, for the sake of propriety, a young man was obliged to wait several weeks before approaching the young lady of his choice. Only then, perhaps, they might take a buggy ride together, but they would almost certainly be accompanied by a chaperon for many frustrating weeks.

However, like all the Grande women, Laura had an independent spirit. While she was visiting her cousin she was keen to adapt to the more informal ways of the West. Even so, going out alone with a man she had only just met was a big step, but there could be no denying she had already begun to like Matt.

43

He was so different to the few boys she had known in Boston. He seemed so confident and self-assured although there was not the slightest trace of arrogance in his manner. So, after taking a deep breath, she replied.

'I'd love to see the range, if Matt is willing to take me.'

'Good,' said Mrs Grande before Matt could answer. 'I'll get the cook to pack you a picnic.'

The cook had been at the ranch for several years. Although Elizabeth and Mrs Grande had only been at the ranch for a few days, they knew better than to interfere with the running of the kitchen again. The giant Chinese cook was brilliant at his job but sulked if anyone else cooked or prepared food in what he considered to be his kitchen. He was still in a bad mood because he had not been allowed to cook last night's meal so, for the sake of a little peace, they allowed him to prepare the picnic basket.

While Laura changed into her best travelling clothes, Elizabeth ordered the ranch's young Mexican wrangler, Paulo, to sort out a suitable horse for the buggy. While it was being harnessed, Luke took Matt to one side and showed him how to use the Henry.

'You probably won't need it,' said Luke, 'but I'd

44

feel better if you took it and the spare box of shells I've already made up.'

It was late morning before Matt and Laura eventually set out. Apart from the Henry and a box of ammunition, they had the most enormous hamper filled to overflowing with food. Matt could not help a rueful grin. Laura asked him to share the joke.

'There's more food in the back of the buggy than we had on our patrols during the Civil War and then there were usually about a dozen of us,' he replied.

'The fighting must have been very frightening,' said Laura, shivering at the thought of Matt being shot at, or engaged in hand-to-hand combat on some bloody battlefield.

Matt tried to reassure her.

'It wasn't that bad. I was attached to the Cavalry. When the Yankees got too close, we had shotguns instead of sabres and that certainly discouraged them; when we were too heavily outnumbered, we simply rode away. Fortunately, our horses were usually faster than theirs!'

Matt's attempted humour did not deceive Laura for a second. She could only guess at the horrors he had been through. The thought sent another shiver right through her.

It was still early spring and the north wind was surprisingly cool. Matt assumed Laura was shivering because she was cold. Most Texans were noted for their gallantry and any Texan worthy of the name would place his free arm around his girl to keep her warm. Of course, Laura wasn't his girl, neither was he a Texan. In spite of her strict Boston upbringing and although she wasn't cold, she didn't object. Quite the opposite: she cuddled into him.

They met no one on the way to the picnic, which was just as well, for Matt only had eyes for Laura, something which she could not fail to notice. After a few miles, they stopped near a solitary clump of pine trees. They were the last few of what had once been a sizable wood, but most of the pines had long since been cut down. Of course, it was from the original wood that the valley and the ranch had got its name.

By the time they had unpacked the hamper, the wind had moderated and it was pleasantly warm. The picnic itself was a great success: the Chinese cook had packed enough beef and chicken to feed a multitude and there was an ample supply of bread, freshly baked before dawn that morning and cakes of every description. Matt could not remember the last time he had eaten so well.

In spite of the need for vigilance, Matt's attention continually returned to Laura. She was the most delightful companion: intelligent, quick-witted and stunningly beautiful. As he began to get know her better, he found there was much more to her than that but he thought he must be imagining the interest she appeared to be taking in him. Nevertheless, her warmth and complete honesty began to induce emotions which he had never allowed himself to feel.

But he had to remind himself that she was only here on an extended holiday and would return back East before long. He also had to remind himself that the War had reduced him to a ranch hand. Not that there was anything wrong in that, in fact, he enjoyed the life. But a girl of Laura's refined upbringing was unlikely to have anything but a passing interest in a dollar-a-day cowboy, or so he thought, but he didn't think to ask her.

On the way back to the Pine Valley ranch, instead of just concentrating on Laura, Matt tried to keep an eye on the trail and the range around them. So this time, he noticed small numbers of unbranded longhorns haphazardly dotted all over the Panhandle. There were only two or three in each group but all of them were grazing on the unpalatable looking sagebrush: it reminded Matt of something he had learnt from his spell at the JT ranch.

It was late in the afternoon by the time they returned to the ranch. Several young Mexicans, some of them women, were working industriously. It was clear that they had been given orders to smarten up the place. They appeared to be willing workers, but vaqueros they were not. Only Paulo, the youthful wrangler, seemed happy around horses and even he was not wearing a six-gun.

Matt left the buggy in the capable hands of the young Mexican. Somehow, he found himself walking arm in arm with Laura into the dining room, where Mrs Grande was already serving coffee. She looked hard at Laura; her steady gaze was met with a blushing smile from her niece, the meaning of which was lost to Matt but not to Mrs Grande.

Mr Grande returned just before dinner. Usually an open and honest man, this time he was different. His manner was distinctly furtive as he ordered several Mexicans to unload the wagon. The wagon was old and battered. Its rear right wheel was out of line and strangely askew leaving a distinctive and wobbly track behind it.

The battered old wagon gave every appearance of being overloaded, yet it seemed to be only carrying dress or curtain material. That was strange because Luke had said the town, Cottonfields, was many days' journey away. So where had Mr Grande bought the material? However, before he could enquire, Mrs Grande interrupted the proceedings and firmly ordered her husband to change out of his trail-stained clothes.

'Jeremiah!' she said crossly. 'Be quick, you know how cook hates us to keep dinner waiting.'

'Sometimes I wonder who runs this place?' he grumbled.

'Well, dear,' replied Mrs Grande. 'If the cook leaves before we return to our own ranch and Elizabeth and I have to do the cooking, do you want to guess who will be doing the washing up?'

He didn't want to guess and so obediently followed his wife into the ranch house. However, his actions were only to create a diversion, for as soon as Mrs Grande was safely inside, the Mexicans hurriedly broke open the false bottom of the wagon and removed several well hidden oblong crates and some smaller square boxes. From their exertions, the crates appeared to be heavy and the boxes, although smaller, seemed to be even heavier.

While Mr Grande kept his wife occupied with

idle chit-chat, the boxes were taken into Luke's private study. He continued with the small talk until he was sure that the job had been completed and then hurried off to change.

Not wishing to incur the wrath of his wife he completed his ablutions as quickly as possible and, dressed in one of his more colourful shirts, hurriedly made his way to the dining room. Even though the ranch belonged to Luke, Mr Grande sat down at the head of the large table. In spite of his haste, he was only just in time: dinner was served seconds later.

The main course was roast pork. As there were no pigs on the ranch, Matt was again puzzled: where had the meat had come from? But there was another greater mystery. Clearly, the ranch was not yet generating any income and as far as he was aware, Texas banks were only issuing credit to ranches now in the possession of Yankee carpetbaggers. Yet he could not believe that Luke had accumulated enough money in his bounty hunting days to run Pine Valley in such a grand manner.

So where was the money coming from to pay for the Chinese cook, the food and provisions and the Mexicans now eating in the bunkhouse? From Mr Grande, perhaps? Yet however informal and friendly the atmosphere in the dining room, there was an unwritten code of conduct in the West which precluded Matt from asking his host any questions on these subjects.

Over the dinner table, Mrs Grande asked her husband how his trip had gone. Unusually, Mr Grande was evasive and swiftly changed the subject by beginning a debate on the fate of the rustled cattle. But were all Pine Valley's longhorns actually missing? As a result of the observations he had made during the return from the picnic, Matt didn't think so.

'Luke, may I ask you the size of your ranch?'

'Certainly, Matt. The extent of the range legally ours is about fifteen hundred acres. We also expected to find about the same number of cattle of which approximately two hundred should have been carrying our brand.'

'Well, most of the branded longhorns have probably been rustled,' said Matt, 'but the unbranded ones are still there. I saw a few dozen of them this afternoon.'

'Where?' said Luke. 'I searched our entire range and counted nothing like that number.'

Matt smiled. Luke came from the wealthy side of the family and that wealth had resulted in him receiving a far better education. As a result, during

51

their youth, Luke had always been the leader. Now, Matt knew something that Luke didn't and that knowledge might be important.

'I guess none of us can claim to be expert ranchers,' he said, 'but I've been a ranch-hand long enough to learn a few things.'

He paused for dramatic effect; except for Mrs Grande, he had everyone's full attention. She was watching Laura who seemed to be transfixed by Matt's words.

'For instance?' asked Luke.

'The difference between how many head of cattle per acre the prairie grass around Redrock and the same area of sagebrush in the Texas panhandle can feed.'

'Which is?' interrupted Laura, unable to remain silent.

'Most Texas ranches allow for only three head of cattle for each hundred acres of sagebrush,' was Matt's astonishing reply.

'But that means our cattle would need at least thirty thousand acres to feed themselves,' said Mrs Grande, now fully focused on Matt.

'That would be the absolute minimum,' agreed Matt.

'But we couldn't afford to buy even another hundred acres!' exclaimed Elizabeth indignantly.

'Of course not. You already own as much as some of the largest ranches in Texas.'

'Sorry Matt, I don't understand,' said Luke.

'Providing no other ranch is already doing so, you don't have to own the land to graze cattle on it. But you do have to be able to stop anybody else claiming them.

'How do we do that?' asked Luke.

'First, hire enough young cowboys to round up and brand at least a thousand longhorns and then drive them to one of the rail head towns like Abilene or Dodge. While that herd is on the trail, you will need more cowboys to brand as many more longhorns as you can – say another thousand steers for the next drive and as many cows as possible to start breeding.'

'But Matt, what are longhorns and where do *we* get them from?' asked Laura.

'Longhorns are wild cows and there are millions, just for the taking, here on the Texas panhandle,' said Matt failing to grasp the significance of Laura's slip of the tongue.

However, Mrs Grande noticed that Laura had said *we* and looked sharply at her niece. The faintest of blushes spread across Laura's cheeks. Matt, of course, failed to notice the byplay.

'But don't these longhorns belong to

somebody?' asked Luke.

'They belong to whoever put their brands on them. Longhorns have been running free and breeding all over the panhandle since the War of Texas Independence and maybe before that for all I know,' replied Matt.

'So we just take them and put our own brand on them?' asked Mrs Grande, doubt written all over her face.

'Why not? If you don't some other rancher will. But then, you will need to put down your markers on the extra thousands of acres of land you will need to feed them. For sure, it will be very hard work and that's the easy part: protecting your new range and keeping your new herd from rustlers, Indians and even other ranches – that will be the real problem.'

'But how could we protect so much land and the cattle on it?' asked Laura looking at Matt.

Again, instinctively, she had said *we* whilst looking at Matt and again Mrs Grande looked at her sharply. This time Elizabeth also noticed the connection between her cousin's words and her glance towards Matt but, as before, he remained oblivious to the interactions and continued speaking.

'Once you have established yourself here, you

will need to hire professional gunmen. But they don't come cheaply.'

'Why gunmen?' asked Laura aghast at the prospect.

'And where is the money to come from?' asked Elizabeth, practical as ever.

'Because west of the Pecos, there's no law. So you may have to fight to keep the ranch.'

The colour drained out of Laura's face. An Easterner, she was not accustomed to the idea of gunfighting; the rest of the Grande family, however, had faced a long and bloody battle to keep their home in Redrock.

During that fighting, Elizabeth had learnt that her father had once been a noted gunfighter. Years of respectable living had not slowed the speed of his gun hand or lessened his determination to use a six-gun to defend his home and loved ones. Without asking, she knew her father would do so again, if the occasion demanded it.

CHAPTER SIX

Next morning, whilst Mrs Grande and the girls were sorting through the dress material her husband had somehow managed to purchase during his mysterious trip, Mr Grande ushered Matt and Luke into his private study. Surprisingly, he took a chisel and hammer with him.

The large oblong crates had been placed on the table which occupied the centre of the study. On the floor by the crates were the smaller square shaped boxes which also appeared to be unopened.

Mr Grande asked Luke to lock the study door and then began to chisel open the first crate. From the ease with which its lid came off, Matt guessed it had been opened before – possibly it had been closed up again to keep prying eyes from seeing its content. His host's next words confirmed his suspicions:

'Until it's absolutely necessary, I don't want my wife or the girls to know I've bought these,' he said pulling out a brand new carbine from the box.

Still covered in its original preservative oil, the carbine was like nothing Luke or Matt had ever seen. Nevertheless, they both knew that it was Colt's revolutionary new Winchester .44 carbine. Like the far longer-barrelled Henry rifle, the Winchester had a lever action and was, therefore, a repeater rifle. Its magazine could hold up to thirteen bullets, all of which could be fired in the time it took to re-load the old single shot Springfield musket rifle.

However, it was its new kind of ammunition which made the Winchester such a revolutionary weapon. Gone was the self-made, roll-your-own, and therefore potentially unreliable, bullet. In its place, was an infinitely superior, factory made, higher velocity cartridge. The heavy square boxes beside the crate contained this new ammunition.

Although stories that a revolutionary new carbine had been around for a couple of years, until now, none had been reported west of the Pecos – yet Mr Grande had been able to purchase ten of them.

'So how did you come by them?' asked Luke.

'From Señor Mendez, Paulo, my young wrangler's uncle. He runs a decent sized spread on the Mexican side of the Rio Grande. He too has been losing cattle and was tracking them when he and his men came upon a couple of heavily laden wagons. They had been trying to cross the Rio Grande but got bogged down. Paulo's uncle soon discovered the reason: hidden under piles of dress and curtain material were half a dozen crates of whiskey.'

'But they wouldn't be heavy enough to cause the wagon to get bogged down,' protested Matt.

'That's what Paulo's uncle thought,' replied Mr Grande. 'So in spite of the driver's objections they took the wagons apart and discovered they both had false bottoms. One wagon carried Winchesters and the ammunition for them was in the other one.'

'What happened to the drivers?' asked Matt.

'All Paulo's uncle would say on that subject was that the wagon drivers wouldn't be gun running again.'

'Matt, do you think there's any connection between the rustling and the gun runners?'

'I doubt it,' replied Matt. 'There have been rumours about gun runners ever since I arrived at the JT ranch, but cattle rustling only started up a few months ago. But there is one thing about the rustling I don't understand.'

'What's that?' asked Mr Grande.

'In Texas, the owners of the big ranches hang rustlers. So if somebody just wanted cattle, why not take unbranded longhorns? I believe whoever is behind the gun running is also out to ruin your ranch and perhaps the JT ranch as well.'

'Why?' asked Mr Grande.

'Sorry, I haven't worked that bit out yet,' admitted Matt ruefully.

Luke remembered that Masters had been the name of one of the raiders killed in the attack on the old adobe line cabin. And Colonel Masters had been the architect of the range war in Redrock. Was there a connection?

A sharp rap at the door interrupted Luke's deliberations. It was Mrs Grande and it was clear she was not happy to find the study door locked.

'Jeremiah!' she called angrily through the locked door. 'Finish your private discussions and put away whatever it is you don't want me to see. We are about to have a visitor and I think he's been wounded.'

Mr Grande hastily returned the Winchester to the crate and unlocked the study door. He hurried outside, followed by Matt and Luke, to see what had so alarmed his wife. They were just in time to see the arrival of a heavily armed Mexican rider. From the way he was slumped over his saddle, it was clear that Mrs Grande had been correct – the vaquero had been badly hurt.

Luke ordered Elizabeth and Laura back into the ranch house, much to Elizabeth's annoyance. Mr Grande and Matt hurried over to the injured rider. The ever practical Mrs Grande got the first aid box and, in spite of Luke's protests, carried it over to the wounded man. However, it took her only a second to discover the Mexican's wounds were beyond her aid; she helped her husband ease the stricken man out of the saddle and on to the sun-baked earth.

The first bullet had struck the vaquero's ribcage but had been almost spent by the time it hit so had not penetrated it. If that had been the Mexican's only injury, it would have been a relatively simple matter to dig the bullet out.

Sadly, it had been the second bullet which had caused the real damage: fired from behind and from a much closer range, it had hit the Mexican in the middle of his back. The severity of the wound would have felled a less determined man, yet somehow, the vaquero had managed to make it to the Grandes' ranch. Loss of blood had made him critically weak but he was still able to tell his story even though his life forces were rapidly ebbing away.

'We are from California. I and several more vaqueros were escorting my master and his lady to his cousin's estate on the Conchos River when we were ambushed near two great peaks.'

'That will be Twin Buttes,' said Matt.

'The driver of the coach was killed and I was hit,' continued the vaquero. 'I managed to drive the coach into a canyon and got it safely behind a rocky outcrop but it was a blind canyon and our attackers occupied the only way out of it. However, we were well prepared and had enough guns and ammunition to hold them off for at least a few days.'

Blood trickled out of the Mexican's mouth causing him to cough. But somehow he managed to continue, although his voice was much weaker.

'Even in California, most people consider my master to be very wealthy. If you save him, I'm sure he will reward you well.'

'We don't take money for helping people in trouble,' said Mr Grande sharply. 'Now if you can give us directions to the exact position your party was ambushed, we will be on our way to rescue them within the hour.'

But there was no answer: the valiant vaquero was dead. Luke instructed his Mexicans to bury him well out of sight of the ranch house but unfortunately, although his body was to be treated with dignity, there was no priest to sanctify the burial.

Elizabeth and Mrs Grande had witnessed death before. In the bloodshed at their previous home in Redrock, one of their young hands had been brutally murdered and then Luke had outdrawn a notorious gunslinger right in front of them. Although those experiences didn't make the death of the vaquero any easier to stomach, at least they were a little more prepared for it than Laura. She burst into tears and began to shake uncontrollably.

Work, not sympathy, was Mrs Grande's remedy. She sent Laura, supervised by Elizabeth, to fetch provisions. She knew, without asking, the men would ride to the rescue of the dead vaquero's master. Laura set to work with such a will that within the hour, the pack horses had been loaded with food, blankets and several canteens full of water.

While the women were still occupied with the preparations for the rescue party, Mr Grande went into the ranch house. After a few minutes, he returned laden with his Henry, a couple of the new Winchester rifles and several boxes of ammunition.

Before they left, Elizabeth and Mrs Grande passionately embraced their respective husbands. As Matt waited for them to complete their goodbyes, an ashen-faced Laura slowly approached him.

'I know you have to go, but you will take care, won't you Matt. I would hate anything to happen to you.'

Notwithstanding her prudish Eastern upbringing, she kissed him gently, but then stepped back too quickly for Matt to respond. Astounded by her unexpected but far from unwanted actions, Matt stood riveted to the spot, but only for a second.

'Could I take another try at that?' he asked her.

She was in his arms in a second. This time there was no holding back and they were still locked in a passionate embrace long after the married couples had finished theirs.

'Seems you two have gotten pretty well acquainted. I guess I must have missed that happening,' said Luke drily as he mounted Josh. The jet black stallion whinnied as if in agreement.

'So where are the Twin Buttes?' asked Luke.

'As the crow flies, due south. I've never been there myself but they are a famous land mark so we should have no difficulty in locating them,' replied Matt.

Although the pack horses slowed them down, the beasts of burden were able to sustain long periods of cantering before they had to rest. Consequently, they reached Twin Buttes at sunset.

Matt was right. The area was so called because it was dominated by two huge columns of rocks which rose vertically into the sky and towered over a boulder-strewn, barren landscape.

The sound of gunfire was amplified by the twin peaks and echoed for miles making its origin difficult to locate. Nevertheless, Luke unerringly led the rescue party to a high ridge: far below them they witnessed a desperate scene.

It seemed that the dead vaquero had driven his master's coach into a blind canyon. Sheltering behind a rockfall from the massive and impenetrable cliff which formed the dead end of the blind canyon were the surviving members of his party. Clearly they had put up a spirited resistance for on the canyon floor between the coach party and the open end of the canyon lay several bodies. It seemed the attackers had paid a heavy price for trying to rush the coach party.

However, the coach party were safe only as long as the attackers remained on the floor of the canyon. If they managed to climb to the top of the canyon's sheer sides, they would be able to direct their fire directly down on to the coach party. Luke wondered why the attackers had so far not tried to do so – apparently their leader preferred to lay siege to the coach party – but Luke was not so patient and he began to devise a plan.

The bandits' slow and ragged rate of fire indicated they were still using rifle muskets. Mr Grande was detailed to count the gun flashes and thus determine how many of them were attacking the coach. He had just finished counting as night fell and all firing ceased.

Would the bandits use the cover of darkness to rush the coach party? Loud and mocking voices continually directed at the coach party by the bandits suggested to Luke they would not.

So before the moon had risen, he made his way along the top of the canyon until he found a steep and narrow path which led down to its floor. As silent as a ghost, he descended. The bandits failed to detect him, proving he had not earned the reputation of being one of the best scouts in the Union army for nothing.

At the foot of the path was another rockfall. Although much smaller than the one behind which the coach party were sheltering, it completely hid

Luke. Before revealing his presence, he checked out the state of the besieged.

During his descent, perhaps unwisely, someone in the coach party had lit a fire. Its flickering flames illuminated the campsite, so had the bandits chosen to rush it under cover of darkness, they would have been silhouetted against its flames, making them easy targets. But no such attack came and even the mocking abuse shouted by the attackers had come to an end.

The camp firelight showed that the coach party had already suffered casualties: a vaquero appeared to be dead while another was obviously seriously wounded. However, he was being expertly attended to by a very well dressed and rather stately Mexican woman.

A Spanish-American boy, also extremely well dressed, was busily reloading a pile of rifle muskets, but Luke could see that their supply of ready-made ammunition had begun to run low. Worse still, their supply of water looked insufficient for them to survive the heat of the canyon floor for more than another day.

Crawlingly silently, Luke reached the encampment, stood up and slowly raised his hands and called softly.

'*Amigos!* Don't shoot, I'm a friend.'

Luke repeated the call until he was sure that the coach party understood. During the Civil War, Luke had seen too many good men mistakenly shot by their own sentries and was not about to risk the same fate.

The well dressed young boy stopped his work and introduced himself in perfect if a little too precise English.

'Señor, I am Fernando Gomez. How you got into this blind canyon I cannot imagine, for as you must have seen, we are trapped in here by bandits. But you are welcome to share my campsite and the little food and water we have.'

'Thank you but no. My friends are waiting for me at the top of the canyon and we have more than enough supplies and water.'

'Then why have you descended into this accursed hellhole, señor?' asked the boy.

'To help you, but could you not have tried to escape past them under cover of the night?' asked Luke.

'Señor, I have wounded who cannot be moved and I will not leave them behind. Besides, the bandits would probably catch up with our coach during the hours of daylight. So we must stay here and fight.'

'But you don't have enough water or

ammunition to survive for more than a day,' said Luke grimly.

'This I know, señor, but I will not surrender. I have sent my best vaquero to get help. We will fight until it arrives or we are all killed,' said Fernando. 'However, this is not your fight, so for your own safety, I urge you to leave.'

Luke explained that before he died, the vaquero had managed to reach the Pine Valley ranch and as a result, Luke and his two friends had come to rescue them.

Fernando's eyes saddened when he learnt of the fate of his vaquero. Luke was surprised to learn that in spite of his tender years, Fernando was the master to whom the dead vaquero had referred and his lady was actually the boy's mother. Indeed, Fernando was the leader of the coach party.

'I thank you for coming to our aid, señor, but what can three men do against so many bandits?' the boy asked.

'You might be surprised. We may be able to give them a nasty shock.'

Luke outlined his plan to Fernando. As there was more than an element of risk, Luke needed the boy's agreement. The youngster readily gave it but there was still much to be done and little time for any further discussion.

Using the shadows created by the moonlight, Luke silently climbed up the canyon's side. During the Civil War he had undertaken similar climbs with ease but that was some years ago and by the time he reached Matt and Mr Grande, much to his cousin's amusement, Luke was badly out of breath.

It was some time before he was able to go through his plan with them. After the details had been agreed, they all rested. There was no need to keep watch; Luke's trail skills had ensured that the bandits were still unaware of their presence.

CHAPTER SEVEN

Just before dawn, they took up their battle positions. Luke stayed on the top of the canyon wall but moved to a site overlooking the beleaguered coach party.

Mr Grande muffled the hoofs of his horse and rode round the canyon's rim, high above its floor. He continued to a point overlooking the bandits' camp on the opposite side of the canyon and then dismounted. Although the journey had taken longer than expected, he was in position by dawn.

Matt and Luke also made their way along the top of the canyon, but on foot. Luke positioned himself on a suitable vantage point overlooking the canyon about half way between the bandits and the coach party.

Matt, however, continued until he came to the

path down to the canyon floor and began to scramble down it. But the descent was not that simple. Designed to be used from horseback, the barrel of his new Winchester carbine was about four inches shorter than that of the Henry rifle. Even so it was still twenty inches long and carrying it down the steep path was far from easy.

At first, he had the moon to guide him. But as he descended, the steep sides of the canyon shut out the moonlight, slowing his progress even more than the need for silence. Consequently, the rays of the early morning sun had almost reached the canyon floor by the time he had reached the cover of the rockfall, behind which Luke had paused a few hours earlier.

The rays of the sun reaching the canyon floor was the signal for the bandits to renew their attack. However, Luke, Matt and Mr Grande remained hidden and at first, did not intervene. As a result, the bandit's fire, which came from too many rifle muskets to count, was returned by only three from the coach party. Yet after only a few minutes, even this weak response ceased.

Nevertheless, the bandits continued to fire at the coach party until they were sure that their victims had either run out of ammunition or were dead. Only then did some of them begin to

71

emerge from behind their rocks and head towards the campsite.

At first, they were cautious, moving from boulder to boulder but as there was still no fire from the campsite they began to walk more openly towards it. This gave Luke the opportunity for which he had planned and he opened fire. His Henry rifle laid down a deadly hail of bullets: two bandits fell, destined never to rise; another was hit but began to crawl back to the safety of his camp. Meanwhile, Luke reloaded his Henry.

As he did so, Mr Grande also opened fire from the opposite side of the canyon: his aim was directed at the bandits still undercover. Their purpose had been to give covering fire if any of their colleagues advancing towards the coach party ran into trouble, but instead, Mr Grande's rapid rate of fire kept them pinned down. The portly ranch owner had no need to reload, for when the Henry was empty, he simply switched to the Winchester carbine he had also taken with him.

The bandits on the canyon floor were cut off. Those nearest the coach party rushed forward but any thoughts they might have had of reaching the safety of the rocks in which the coach party were hidden were dispelled as the surviving vaqueros opened fire again.

There was no quarter for the bandits as a second volley came from the direction of the campsite. Even the injured bandit who had been crawling painfully towards the rocks was hit again. This time he ceased to move.

Although there were only two men and the boy left to fight, they had seven loaded rifle muskets between them and the boy's aunt to help reload them. But only once, for there was no more ammunition. Young Fernando had gambled all on one final volley.

He was right to do so. As two more bandits bit the dust, the rest turned tail and ran back towards their camp. In doing so, they passed close to Matt, still hidden by the outcrop of rocks. At point blank range, Matt opened fire. There wasn't time to check how many he hit but only three bandits made it back to their camp. But there were still many bandits left and they were safely undercover: the coach party was now defenceless.

However, Luke had also planned for this eventuality. While the bandits regrouped, he raced back along the top of the canyon until he found a position which overlooked the campsite. Meanwhile, Matt reloaded his Winchester and moved to a position from which he could more easily defend the coach party. High on the opposite side of the canyon, Mr Grande took advantage of the lull to reload his Henry rifle and Winchester carbine.

Although the rescuers were still heavily out-numbered, the firepower of their repeating rifles gave them the advantage. Moreover, Luke and Mr Grande, now facing each other from the top of the opposite sides of the canyon, had the bandits in a deadly crossfire. So deadly, three more bandits died within the next few minutes.

The rout was almost complete. Almost twenty rifle muskets had proved no match for the combined firepower of three men armed with Winchesters and Henry rifles. Less than an hour after dawn, the surviving bandits threw down their arms and surrendered. The battle of Twin Buttes was over almost as soon as it had started.

In spite of his tender years, Fernando wanted to hang the surviving bandits on the spot, but Matt thought he had a better idea: he released them, but not before they had removed their boots and their six-guns, rifle muskets and horses were confiscated.

Mr Grande insisted that the defeated men were given a couple of canteens of water to share between them. However, later this compassion was to cost him dearly.

Now, barefoot and unarmed, the bandits were obliged to walk away from the battle site. It would take them several days to reach the nearest settlement, during which time they would have only some of the provisions originally packed by Laura and Elizabeth for the rescue party. Also, to hang on to their scalps, they would have to avoid any contact with the Kiowa-Apache.

In fact, the bandits' chances of survival appeared to be slim. But a slim chance of survival was better than dangling on the end of a noose and a much better fate than the one they had intended for the occupants of the coach.

So, in spite of the danger, the bandits willingly set off towards the border – Mr Grande was detailed to follow them. Unused to walking barefoot, the bandits found it very tough going and their profanities filled the air as they stepped on stones hidden in the wiry grass.

Mr Grande shadowed them for several hours before heading back to the campsite at Twin Buttes. Had he followed them across the Rio Grande, he might have been forewarned and a future disaster might have been averted. But, of course, he could not see into the future and he returned to the victorious coach party in time to share in a meal made from the rest of the provisions carried by the pack horses.

During the meal, it was decided that they would stay with the coach party until they found a suitably safe place to cross the Rio Grande. Then Mr Grande and Luke would return to the Pine Valley ranch, taking the bandits' mustangs with them.

Matt and the pack horses would remain with the coach party until they reached the ranchero belonging to Fernando's relatives. This was situated about thirty miles north of Meoqui on the Conchos river.

They started out a little after dawn the next morning. Pulled by a team of six trained horses, the coach made good time. Nevertheless, it was dusk before they reached the Rio Grande. It was decided to camp and look for a suitable place to cross the river in the morning. Although the area seemed deserted and they had seen no sign of the barefoot bandits or Kiowa-Apaches, Luke deemed it to be too risky to light a fire.

It had been a long day and most of them had had little or no sleep the night before, so they were all tired. But as the rest of the party settled down to sleep, Matt and Luke took turns to stand guard. Although they had spared the life of the bandits, both knew they would not hesitate to slaughter the entire coach party if they could sneak undetected

76

into the camp and grab a few guns.

The night past uneventfully but morning found the Rio Grande swollen by the spring rains, making normal fording impossible. So the coach had to be stripped of its load and a raft constructed to carry the luggage and passengers across the mighty river. Sizeable logs would then have to be lashed to the coach to give it extra ballast before, towed by the horses, it too could make the crossing.

However, building a raft substantial enough to carry the luggage, the wounded vaqueros and the boy's mother across the swirling waters of the Rio Grande was no small matter. Several large trees had to be found, felled, and cut up into logs – all this, with just a few fighting axes carried by some of the coach party's vaqueros.

Yet, as difficult as that was, it was only the start of their problems: the logs had to be moved from where they had been cut down to the fording place. It was very hard work and the process took a whole day. Another day was lost in building and loading the raft.

Even then, they were not ready to ford the Rio Grande. More logs had to be cut and lashed to the coach, but the coach refused to float so yet more logs had to be cut. These were also lashed securely to each side of the coach to make it more buoyant.

And it worked, but not before another delay.

Fernando's mother objected strongly as her luggage was unloaded off the coach and her disapproval grew stronger when she discovered that they and herself and her son were to be transported across the Rio Grande on the make-shift raft. For sometime she refused. Although she spoke in Spanish, which Matt did not understand, her arrogant tone suggested that she was not used to having her wishes ignored. But that was precisely what a tired and somewhat grumpy Matt did.

Fortunately, by the time everything was ready for the crossing, the flood waters of the Rio Grande had abated a little. But although the level of the river had fallen, its swirling current remained as strong and deadly as ever.

The coach, driven by a vaquero, was half driven, half floated across the Rio Grande. The raft followed. In front of it rode Matt and Luke each with a rope tied to the pommel of their saddles and attached to each side of the raft. Slowly and carefully, they manoeuvred it away from the bank. Mr Grande steered the raft by means of a crudely constructed rudder.

Josh and Matt's horse, Spike, took up the strain

and began to cross the Rio Grande. But they were soon out of their depth and had to swim. In spite of the swirling current Spike seemed to enjoy the experience and if Josh was afraid he wasn't about to show it in front of Spike.

The crossing was achieved without mishap, but they were all soaked to the skin, so in spite of the danger, this time they lit a fire. Although Fernando's mother still tended the wounded vaquero, she made no attempt to do any cooking. That chore fell to Matt. While he did so, Luke and Mr Grande scouted the trail ahead, but they had little of consequence to report when they returned.

Unaccomplished in the art of cooking, Matt made a stew from rabbits shot by the other vaquero. It was not as good as the one cooked by Luke in the adobe line cabin, but it was at least a warm meal.

Next day, Luke and Mr Grande re-crossed the mighty river and headed homewards. The rest also broke camp but travelled along its Mexican bank. As Matt discussed the unusually high level of the Rio Grande with Fernando, he was rebuked by the boy's mother.

'In Mexico, the great river is called the Rio Bravo del Norte,' she said in perfect English.

Matt was so surprised, he almost fell off his horse.

'Because you are unable to master more than one language, it does not follow that others are so inept,' she said scornfully. 'Indeed, I was born in the French speaking area of Basque. My husband, the Count, was Spanish, so when we married I naturally learnt to speak his language.'

She went on to say that she and her late husband had left Spain when Fernando had been little more than a baby. After a long and perilous sea journey to California and an even more dangerous overland trek, they reached and settled on his family's magnificent estate. It had been run by an aged relative, who had originally settled in California when all of it and Mexico were still under Spanish control.

After a day, the coach party reached the place where the Conchos River flowed into the Rio Grande. At that point, they turned southwards away from the border and then journeyed along the river bank of the Conchos. Unfortunately, in places, the coach had to slow to a crawl because of the rough going.

After a couple of days, they reached a huge wadi but it was still full of spring flood water and its steep sides made crossing it impossible. So they had to continue up the Conchos until they found a suitable place to ford the Spanish river. This time there was no need for rafts. Then, the coach party had to retrace their path back to the wadi before turning eastwards along its bank.

They followed it for many miles until they arrived at the magnificent hacienda of Fernando's cousin. It was called El Chicote and it was surrounded by a huge white adobe stockade complete with fortified ramparts. These were manned and patrolled by a large number of soldiers. Indeed, the hacienda looked and felt more like an army garrison than a ranch.

The area inside the stockade was huge. Apart from the actual hacienda, which was as big as the ranch houses of the JT and Pine Valley ranches put together, the enclosure contained several large buildings and two big corrals.

One of the soldiers spoke English and told Matt that one of the corrals was reserved for use by the Mexican army. However, the other, even larger corral was full of magnificent snow white horses, too many for Matt to count.

The arrival of the coach party occasioned much joy and triggered the betrothal celebrations. Matt's part in the rescue was vividly recounted and greatly exaggerated so much so, he was asked to stay for the wedding. But as the happy event was still several days off, he declined the offer. The rustlers still had to be dealt with and the cattle retaken. So, reluctantly, he left next day with the sound of gratitude ringing in his ears.

CHAPTER EIGHT

It felt too quiet. Something was wrong. No matter how much Matt tried to shake off the feeling, the nearer he got to the Pine Valley ranch, the stronger it became. In the end, it became so overwhelming, he decided to circle the ranch instead of riding straight up to it.

He was almost halfway round his circuit and was beginning to feel very foolish, when he came across a great number of horse tracks. Those leading to the ranch house were widely spaced which suggested to Matt that the horses had been at a full gallop. However, the tracks leading away from the ranch house were spaced much closer together, indicating the horses had only been going at walking pace.

Amongst the tracks leading away from the ranch

house were those of a wagon. They had left deep ruts suggesting that it had been heavily over-loaded. The track left by the left rear wheel was crooked, suggesting the wagon was the one recently used by Mr Grande. A feeling of foreboding overwhelmed Matt.

Perhaps it was only instinct, but something told him not to approach the ranch house openly, so he dismounted and tethered Spike to a nearby shrub. Then, using every piece of cover he could find, he made his way to the ranch house.

His instinct had been right: something was wrong for the ranch house was completely deserted. Or was it? The slightest of noises indicated that somebody was in the barn.

Its door was half open. Matt drew his six-gun and entered cautiously. In front of him was Luke, hog-tied, gagged and lying in a pool of blood. Standing over him was a Mexican, who reached for his six-gun and fired with bewildering speed.

A fatal mistake. His bullet struck the half-open barn door; Matt's bullet struck the Mexican just above his heart, killing him instantly. But the carnage wasn't over yet.

The sound of clinking spurs indicated someone was approaching the barn. Matt took a few steps forward, then turned to face its door. A second

Mexican raced into the barn, six-gun at the ready. Yet not ready enough. Matt's six-gun fired first, its bullet again struck with deadly effect. The Mexican was dead by the time he hit the floor of the barn, given away by his large Mexican spurs.

Matt holstered his six-gun, rushed over to his cousin and undid his gag.

'Nice shooting cousin,' gasped Luke.

'You're covered in blood. Are you hurt?' asked Matt anxiously.

'No. The blood's not mine, it's only my pride that's hurt. After all my years as an army scout, I let myself get taken like a tenderfoot by the Mexicalaros. But that's not the worst: they have taken Elizabeth, the Grandes, and the Mexican workers they didn't kill. We must go after them. I need water and food, but first, get me out of these damned ropes.'

With a knife retrieved from his saddle-bags, Matt cut his cousin free. But at first, Luke was unable to stand. So while his cousin was still helpless, Matt filled a canteen from the horse trough. Luke was too thirsty to be fussy.

Slowly and painfully, Luke's circulation began to return to normal and he managed to stagger to his feet. With Matt's help, he hobbled across the courtyard into the ranch house.

An hour later, Luke, washed and changed, had almost recovered. However, he was famished so began to cook a meal. Meanwhile, Matt unsaddled and groomed his horse. For the last few days, he had ridden Spike hard so now the stallion needed rest.

By the time Matt had finished grooming Spike, the aroma of bacon and fresh laid eggs came from the kitchen. Pursuit being impossible, they ate heartily and Luke began to explain his ordeal.

'Just after dawn, two days ago, they hit us. They reached the kitchen and captured Mrs Grande and the cook before I could organize any proper resistance.'

'Was she hurt?'

'No, but they shot the cook.'

'What about Mr Grande?'

'He was still in bed when the attack came. By the time he had dressed, it was all over.'

'So what happened to you?' asked Matt.

'I was in the barn. I winged two of them but then they captured Elizabeth and Laura. They threatened to shoot them if I didn't surrender, so what could I do?'

Luke looked pleadingly at Matt. The thought of Laura in the hands of the Mexicalaros turned Matt's blood cold, yet he could only guess the torment the loss of his wife was causing his cousin, so sought to reassure him.

'There was nothing you could do. The war taught me that there are times when surviving to fight another day is more important than dying a hero. Dead, what could you do to save your wife?'

Luke looked only a little reassured, but he continued:

'It was agreed that I should try to escape and warn you before you were caught. Nearly got away, but they had riders acting as lookouts and one of them saw me. After that, they hog-tied me and put me in the barn.'

'But what about the blood you were covered in?'

'One of our Mexican lads managed to escape and tried to free me, but they shot him before he could do so, even though he wasn't toting a gun. He fell on top of me. After that, I remember nothing. When I came round, there was no sign of the Mexican but I was covered in his blood and tied up. I was struggling to free myself when one of them came into the barn and saw me. Next minute you arrived.'

'Are you sure they were Mexicalaros?' asked Matt.

'Yes. Some of them were American and openly bragged about it.'

There was nothing to be done that night. Spike needed rest after being ridden hard all day and Luke was in no condition to ride, even if the Mexicalaros had left any horse behind.

Next day found both men fully recovered. While Matt cooked breakfast, Luke looked round his ranch to see what damage the Mexicalaros had done. His findings surprised Matt.

'Little or no damage. They've taken all the horses, including my Josh and about half the food. But they left the two you disposed of to guard the place,' Luke said as he devoured his breakfast.

'Which suggests they aim to return. But did they get any of the Winchesters?'

'No. I had just finished hiding them and their ammunition under the straw in the barn when the Mexicalaros attacked. And they didn't find my other six-gun, a Remington 45. It's a twin of the one they've taken. They are a matched pair, but I always found carrying two six-guns too cumbersome.'

'If I was as good with a six-gun as you, I wouldn't need two, either,' said Matt drily.

'You didn't do too badly yesterday, cousin. However, the Mexicalaros have got both Henry rifles. But they would still be no match for our Winchesters, if only we had a few good men and spare horses to go after them.'

'So what do you suggest we do?' asked Matt.

'Well, one of us must follow them. I can't leave Elizabeth in the hands of that scum.'

'Or Laura,' said Matt without thinking.

His cousin looked at Matt quizzically.

'So that's the way the wind blows. Does she know how you feel?'

'Of course not. Laura is way too good for a dollar-a-day cowboy like me. In any case, even if we do manage to rescue the prisoners, I guess Laura will have had enough of the West and will want to return East as soon as she can.'

'Perhaps. But let's not get ahead of ourselves. With only one horse between us, catching up with the Mexicalaros and releasing the prisoners will be a neat trick. Any ideas?' asked Luke.

The sound of horses galloping rapidly towards the ranch house prevented Matt's reply. In perfect unison, the cousins rose and drew their six-guns. As fast as Luke undoubtedly was, Matt was only fractionally slower.

'Not bad,' said Luke approvingly.

The riders were not Mexicalaros, for leading them was Paulo, the Grandes' young wrangler. With him was a distinguished looking Mexican and three vaqueros leading a string of spare horses.

The riders had not eaten since they camped the previous night; this time, Luke cooked. At the insistence of the distinguished looking Mexican who was Paulo's uncle, the vaqueros ate their meals in the bunkhouse.

In the ranch house, while they ate, Paulo explained how he had escaped.

'I was out on the range, rounding up stray mustangs when the Mexicalaros attacked. Mama forbids me to carry a gun, so without a weapon, there was nothing I could do. So I rode to my uncle's hacienda to ask for help.'

'Juan Mendez at your service. Unfortunately, when Paulo reached my hacienda I was away and didn't return until the following day. Then, of course, we could not leave my home undefended. Making the necessary arrangements took a little time, but we came as soon as we could.'

'I reckon there must be at least two dozen Mexicalaros,' said Luke. 'They have taken my wife, her parents and her cousin, plus several Mexicans who worked here. Will you help us go after them?'

'Of course, señor. Why else are we here? But I thought to leave young Paulo and at least one of my men to watch over your ranch.

'But Uncle, my honour is a stake,' protested Paulo. 'It is my duty to go after these terrible men.

They shot my friends and kidnapped my employers.'

'Paulo, as your guardian, I'll be the judge of your duty,' said his uncle sternly. 'Go tend to the horses. Whatever is decided, nothing can be done until they are groomed, fed and rested.'

Reluctantly, Pedro left to carry out his chores. But his mood soon passed, for he was never happier than when tending to horses. Whilst he did so, his uncle briefed the cousins.

These are perilous times. I regret to inform you that there are even worse dangers in the panhandle than the Mexicalaros.'

'Explain, Señor Mendez, if you please,' asked Luke.

'My information is that the Kiowa-Apaches are on the warpath.'

'Maybe, but I thought the Kiowa-Apaches lived east of the Pecos,' said Matt.

'They did,' said Señor Mendez. 'However, it seems a break-away branch of the Mexicalaros is operating in Kiowa-Apache territory, so the Indians have retaliated by sending war parties west of the Pecos. Unfortunately, that has caused friction with their Apache cousins already living here and at least two Apache sub-chiefs are on the warpath.'

91

'None of which helps us get our folks back,' said Luke testily.

'There I must disagree,' replied Señor Mendez. 'The Mexicalaros are not fools. They know that they cannot survive without the support of the Apaches. I think the kidnapping of your kinfolk is related to that fact.'

'How so? I don't understand,' said Luke.

'I believe that as a sign of good faith, the western Mexicalaros will trade your kinfolk with the Apaches based on the Mexican side of the Rio Grande,' said Señor Mendez.

'What would the Mexicalaros hope to gain from that,' asked Luke.

'The Apaches help in keeping the Kiowa-Apache war parties east of the Pecos,' replied Señor Mendez.

'I shudder to think what will happen to Laura, Elizabeth and the Grandes if they fall into the hands of the Apaches,' said Matt.

'Don't forget the Mexicans, I doubt they would fare any better,' added Luke grimly, even though his main concern was for his wife.

'You're right,' agreed Señor Mendez, 'the men will be tortured and then put to death and most of the women will be absorbed into the tribe as slaves and eventually, if they are lucky, they may become squaws. That is the way of the Indian.'

Mark shuddered at the thought of the eastern born Laura becoming an Indian squaw.

'Then at all costs, we must stop the Mexicalaros from crossing the Rio Grande,' said Luke.

With an effort Matt pulled himself together.

'I guess they will use Desolation Ford for the crossing. From there, it's the shortest distance to the Mexicalaros' stronghold in the mountains,' said Matt.

'In that case, they will probably follow the trail they used when they rustled Pine Valley's cattle,' said Luke. 'But they will be slowed down by the wagon and in any case, it's unlikely they will see any need to hurry.'

'But we can't start until the horses are well rested. Can we still intercept them before they reach the crossing?' asked Señor Mendez.

'I have a plan,' said Matt.

It was a simple plan: to get to Desolation Ford before the Mexicalaros and prevent them crossing into Mexico. Although the Mexicalaros had over two days' head start, it seemed they intended to follow the meandering course of the Rio Grande to Desolation Ford. Matt also hoped their wagonload of prisoners would slow them down and add as much as an extra day to their journey.

To get there before them, Luke, Señor Mendez and one vaquero, together with spare horses would ride directly to the ford. They were armed with the new Winchesters, nevertheless it was decided to delay any attack until Matt arrived with reinforcements.

Matt was to head to the JT ranch but he would not ride alone. After a heated discussion, at the end of which Señor Mendez eventually gave way, it was agreed that Paulo was to ride with him. They too were to take spare horses and the rest of the Winchesters. The remaining two vaqueros would stay at Pine Valley to guard the ranch.

Matt had two reasons for riding to the JT ranch: one was to warn his former boss, Mr Thompson about the Mexicalaros and the Kiowa-Apache war parties. But even if the JT trail hands had not yet returned from Dodge, he hoped to recruit reinforcements from the ranch to help rescue the prisoners. Then, they would ride to Desolation Ford to join forces with Luke's party and attempt to rescue the captives.

Strive as he might, Matt could not get the picture of Laura as a helpless captive out of his mind. Yet he must, for how the rescue was to be achieved without injury or worse to the prisoners, he had absolutely no idea.

94

Although the Mexicalaros had a long lead, by taking a more direct route Luke was confident his party could reach the crossing place before they did. But could Matt do the same? Without him and the reinforcements he hoped to bring from the JT ranch, the plight of the prisoners looked hopeless.

CHAPTER NINE

An hour before dawn, the rescue parties breakfasted. Then, in spite of the pouring rain, they loaded up the saddled bags of pack horses with provisions and ammunition for the Winchesters.

The chase was on. However, far from being a problem, the non-stop rain helped to keep the galloping horses refreshed. By riding hard and frequently changing horses, a rain-soaked Matt and a bedraggled Paulo reached the JT ranch in the early hours of the following morning, much to the astonishment of Mr Thompson.

The very fact that they had ridden up to the ranch house unchallenged concerned Matt gravely. What if there had been a Kiowa-Apache raiding party or the Mexicalaros? In spite of the late hour, Mrs Thompson, still in her night attire, prepared a hot supper for them. In front of a blazing log fire, Matt recounted all that had happened.

'Your tidings are far worse than I feared,' said Mr Thompson gravely.

'Can you help?' asked Matt. 'We have spare Winchester carbines but nobody to use them.'

Mr Thompson thought for several moments before answering.

'Unfortunately, the trail herders are not yet back from Dodge and I must leave some trail hands to guard the ranch house. But however few we may be in number, the JT ranch will ride to help a neighbour in such dire need.'

Nothing more could be done that night, so Matt was glad to accept an invitation to sleep in the guest room while Paolo was more than content to bed down in the bunk house.

There was no such respite for Luke's party. Even if it had been safe to do so, it was too wet to light a fire or even sleep, so, as soon as the horses were sufficiently rested, they rode on in the pouring rain.

They spent an equally unpleasant morning riding to Desolation Ford. However, to avoid any chance of detection, they covered the last few miles cautiously, with Luke scouting the trail ahead. As a result, the ford was not reached until mid afternoon.

Unfortunately, in spite of Luke's earlier confidence, they were too late: on ground made soft by the torrential rain, the trail left by the crooked wagon wheel led directly into the Rio Grande. Luke judged the wagon tracks to be no more than an hour or so old. Otherwise, the never ending, torrential rain would have washed them away.

On either side of the wagontracks there were signs it was being escorted by many horsemen. So many, that without reinforcements, any attempt at rescue must be doomed to failure.

Yet the fear of the rain washing out all tracks prompted Luke to urge the others to cross the Rio Grande immediately. But his usually impeccable judgement was clouded by his love for his wife and desperate concern for the rest of the Grande family. Fortunately, wiser council prevailed:

'No, my amigo, we cannot ride further,' said Señor Mendez firmly. 'The horses are exhausted and we are too tired to think clearly. We must wait for Señor Matt and hope he brings reinforcements.'

Unfortunately, as bad as the weather now was, it

became even worse; the wind changed to the north quarter and then began to blow more strongly. Even though it was spring, the temperature dropped extremely rapidly and in a way that was unique to the open ranges of the West. Ice cold rain now lashed into their faces.

'We must get out of this rain,' said Señor Mendez, water streaming from his face in spite of his Mexican style hat.

'You're right. There's nothing to be gained by waiting here at the ford. I know where there's a line cabin where we can shelter.'

Señor Mendez did not need a second invitation and Luke led them to the big adobe line cabin in which he and Matt had been attacked.

While the vaquero tended to the horses, Luke shed his rain gear and lit the kitchen fire. However, there was to be no rest for the vaquero: after he had settled the horses down, Señor Mendez ordered him to light a fire and then cook a meal. Meanwhile, he and Luke went into the main room and began to discuss what to do next.

Unfortunately, cooking was not one of the vaquero's main attributes and the meal consisted only of beans and hard tack. But his coffee was good. The vaquero then excused himself and returned to the kitchen, partly to keep watch from its window but mostly because Señor Mendez did not permit his vaqueros to eat with him.

While they were eating, Señor Mendez voiced the concern which had been bothering him since the outset of their rescue mission.

'Even if Señor Matt brings many reinforcements, I still cannot see how rescue of the prisoners can be accomplished safely. If we attack in force, no matter how many Mexicalaros we kill, the rest will surely shoot the prisoners before we can reach them.'

Throughout their journey, Luke had been toying with the same problem, but so far, he had not come up with the answer. He could only hope his cousin had done better.

'Señor Mendez, I think it is better to wait for Matt to arrive before making any plans. At least then we will know how many men we will have.'

They didn't have long to wait: soon after the north wind abated and the rain stopped, Matt's party arrived.

'I guessed I'd find you sheltering in the old adobe line cabin,' said Matt as Luke brought him up to date with the news.

Matt's party included Mr Thompson, three JT ranch hands and Paulo, but that made only nine of them in all. Clearly, there were not enough of them for an all-out attack.

While Paulo tended to the horses and Señor Mendez's vaquero cooked still more beans, a council of war was called. However, after an hour of intense discussions, no new plan emerged, so, exhausted after riding all day, they all turned in.

Bright sunlight, and the smell of cooking bacon, awoke Matt. It was Paolo's turn to make breakfast and he had found some more provisions. There was no sign of Luke, and his horse was no longer tethered outside the cabin, but they returned just after everyone else had finished breakfast.

'Hope you've saved me some,' he said.

'Sure have,' replied Mr Thompson, 'but where have you been?'

'Across the Rio Grande. Fortunately, the rain had not washed the wagon tracks away; its rickety back wheel finally gave way, so the Mexicalaros weren't able to reach the safety of their hills. They've camped near a group of cottonwoods about ten miles or some on the other side of the Rio Grande. Behind the trees runs a dry gulley, yet they haven't posted any guards, so I guess they must feel pretty safe.'

'Did you see any of the prisoners?' asked Matt anxiously.

'Mr Grande's workers were tied up but I

couldn't risk letting them see me in case their surprise gave me away.'

'What about the rest?' asked Matt anxiously.

'No sign of them. But it was still very early and no one was stirring, so I guess they could still have been in the wagon. It's not going anywhere until they get a new wheel, so breakfast if you please.'

On cue, Paulo brought a huge plate of bacon and beans out of the kitchen.

'Matt, while I'm eating, give a Winchester to Mr Thompson and another one to whoever else you think is the best shot. Leave the other three here – we may need them later.'

'Then I take it you have a plan, cousin?' asked Matt.

'Well, their campsite has given me an idea but the details can wait until I've eaten.'

In fact, on the way back from the Mexicalaros' camp, Luke had devised a plan. Now they knew the whereabouts of all the Mexicalaros, there was no need for the hacienda of Señor Mendez to remain so heavily guarded so part of Luke's plan was to send Paulo back there for reinforcements. Luke didn't doubt that Paulo would jump at the opportunity to prove his worth, but would his uncle agree to his young nephew making such a long and dangerous journey alone?

Luke outlined his plan, such that it was. It was clear enough up to the point of the actual rescue but after that, there were too many variables to produce a detailed plan. From then on, they would have to play it by ear.

As Luke had anticipated, his plan met with strong opposition from Señor Mendez. Luke let him have his say for a little while and then interrupted:

'Has anyone else got a better plan?' he asked.

There was complete silence.

'Very well then. The time for debate is over. Let's saddle up and get riding. You too Paulo. Bring as many men back to the old cabin as quickly as you can. Before long we may need all the help we can get.'

CHAPTER TEN

The Mexicalaros could not move on until the wagon's wheel had been replaced so a raiding party set out in search of a replacement or to steal another wagon. The rest hobbled their mustangs in front of an unusually large clump of cottonwoods about a hundred or so paces away from their campsite. The wagon was situated about twenty paces in front of the remuda.

There was little for the Mexicalaros to do but wait so to keep his men happy their leader agreed to share out part of the rot-gut whiskey stored in the old wagon along with the Pine Valley prisoners. One unlucky man had been delegated to remove the saddles from their mustangs and stand watch over them but at least he had a bottle of rye whiskey to keep him company.

However, good whiskey requires several years to mature. This whiskey wasn't even that many weeks old. Known as fire-water by the Indians or moonshine back in Louisiana, this load had originally been destined for the Apaches as a gesture of goodwill. But now, the Mexican workers captured at Pine Valley were to take their place.

As Luke had guessed, the old wagon had also become the temporary home and prison for the Grande family en route to the headquarters of the Mexicalaros. But the old wagon had hit a deep rut; the impact, plus the combined weight of the prisoners and whiskey had proved too much for its already weakened rear wheel.

Behind the cottonwoods and out of sight of the Mexicalaros, ran a dry gulley. It was this gulley which had been the inspiration for Luke's rescue plan and along it he now crawled followed by Matt and one of Señor Mendez's vaqueros.

As they reached the cottonwoods, Luke signalled his companions to stop and then cautiously clambered out of the gulley. Using the trees as cover, he moved silently towards the remuda.

It was a mark of the overconfidence of the Mexicalaros that they had only posted one man to unsaddle the horses and watch over the remuda.

However, it seemed that the guard had other things on his mind.

First, he drank deeply from his bottle of whiskey. Then, his attention was distracted by his failure to light a cigareet, a type of thin cigar rolled from black tobacco. Possibly, the tobacco was still damp from yesterday's rain, but whatever the cause, no matter how many times the bandit tried, the cigareet refused to light.

Silent as Luke had been, his horse Josh, held captive in the remuda, detected him. Because of the way the Mexicalaros habitually mistreated their own horses, the stallion had already formed a deep hatred for them, so he whinnied, then reared several times as he detected the presence of his true master. The stallion's unexpected reaction startled the guard and he whirled round to see what had startled the beast. But he saw nothing untoward, so continued to try to light his cigareet only to encounter the same lack of success.

The Mexican's preoccupation with his cigareet proved to be his undoing: it was still unlit as Luke moved silently from behind the cover of a large cottonwood and drove his knife into the hapless guard's back. The Mexican died instantly.

Luke caught his lifeless body and lowered it noiselessly to the ground. He detested killing anyone in this manner, although he had done so on more than one occasion during the Civil War. Yet this time, he felt little remorse: if their positions had been reversed the Mexican would not have hesitated to kill him. Besides, nothing was going to stop him rescuing his beloved Elizabeth and the rest of the prisoners.

Luke signalled to the vaquero that all was clear. Señor Mendez's right hand man climbed out of the gulley and quickly donned the dead man's hat and coat. Then, purely out of habit, he stooped to retrieve the dead guard's cigareet and lit it at the first attempt. The vaquero calmly took the place of the dead guard while Luke dragged the unfortunate man's body away and hid it in the cottonwoods.

Even allowing for their revels, which were now in full swing, at least one of the Mexicalaros might have noticed Luke's actions. However, their attention was riveted on the approach of three riders, one of them leading a saddled but riderless horse.

Yet it was the Winchester carbine, which the first of the riders held above his head, that grabbed the interest of the Mexicalaros leader who stood up to greet the unexpected arrivals. Surprisingly, he was an American. Luke, again hidden behind the cottonwoods, recognized the man instantly.

Luke had kept some of the more important Wanted notices he had used during the time he was a bounty hunter. Amongst them were several for the leader of the Mexicalaros. Known only as Drago, Wanted notices for his capture, dead or alive, had been issued for him in Missouri, Kansas and Texas. The combined rewards exceeded fifteen hundred dollars.

As a result, Drago had been top of Luke's wanted list during his last months as a bounty hunter. Although he had tried to track the outlaw down, each time he had got close to him, Drago had somehow managed to give him the slip. Tracking a known associate of the outlaw had taken him to Redrock and it was there he first met Elizabeth.

Luke was abruptly brought back to the present by the cold and deadly tone of Drago's greeting.

'You are either a very brave or a very foolish man to enter my camp with so few companions,' he said.

'My name is Juan Mendez and I am neither brave nor foolish. Just a gun dealer with something very special to sell.'

With that, he tossed the Winchester carbine to Drago. The American examined it closely. That he was impressed was certain, but he scowled darkly as he discovered the carbine was unloaded. However, he recovered rapidly and a sly look quickly replaced the scowl.

'Señor, I am forgetting my manners,' he said with forced politeness. 'Will you and your men dismount and take some refreshment. Then we can discuss business.'

Señor Mendez smiled but neither he nor any of his vaqueros made any attempt to dismount. Instead, he coolly addressed the American:

'Mr Drago, only a fool would ride into the camp of the Mexicalaros with carbines and ammunition. But if we can make a satisfactory deal, in a short time, you shall have as many of both as you need.'

'Amigo, I have no other name but Drago. But tell me, what is to stop me from shooting you and taking the carbine? I'm sure your compatriots can be persuaded to tell me where they are hidden,' said the outlaw drawing his six-gun.

'Another Winchester, loaded and pointing at your chest might stop you, señor.'

The vaquero who had taken the place of the dead Mexicalaro guarding the remuda, now pointed a Winchester at Drago.

'If you wish for a test, just keep your six-gun aimed at me,' continued Señor Mendez as if he

109

were talking to one of his vaqueros. 'I'm sure your men will be impressed by the Winchester's rapid rate of fire. It will give them something to talk about while they bury you and anyone who tries to help you.'

'But señor, you will also be dead.'

'Only if your trigger finger is faster than my marksman and he has been specially selected and trained for this very moment,' bluffed Señor Mendez calmly.

With a dry laugh, Drago holstered his six-gun, but as he did so, almost imperceptibly, he nodded at one of his henchmen. The man, also an American, rose casually, and then began to make his way towards the wagon containing the prisoners. If Señor Mendez noticed he gave no indication, but Luke, now using the remuda for cover, also began to head for the old wagon.

'You seem to have thought out this meeting very well,' continued Drago. 'But I like that. Perhaps we may do business, after all. What do you propose?'

'I can get forty Winchester carbines and enough ammunition to last for many weeks to you by the end of the month. The total package will cost you two thousand dollars.'

'Señor, even if I had the money, I could buy enough Springfields to equip an army for that.'

'But you would have to feed and pay them. Forty Winchesters will give you enough fire power to destroy any patrol or war party you may encounter.'

'Nevertheless, señor, it's still a great deal of money for something I haven't seen in action.'

'Well, I have a couple more stashed away quite near here. Perhaps you would care to try one of them?'

'Señor, as I expect you know, there is a price on my head. So I'm careful with whom I ride and to where I ride.'

'Since when can a Mexican ride into any Texas town to claim bounty on an American?' asked Señor Mendez, apparently still as calm as ever.

'Well, perhaps you're right. If you will tell your man to put down his Winchester, I will follow you. But not alone and if you are intending to lead us into a trap, be assured you will be the first to die.'

It was not an empty threat. Drago was no fool, and years on the outlaw trail had made him very wary. Indeed, he now regretted he had not posted more than one guard. His instinct told him that Mendez was not on the level but he would not be caught out again.

Once the vaquero had lowered his Winchester, he no longer posed any threat. Indeed, Drago was of a mind to order his men to shoot the vaquero and the trader calling himself Mendez, but forty Winchesters, that was some prize! So he was willing to play along with Mendez, at least for the time being, but his mind was already working on a plan of his own.

Drago chose three men to join him, while the vaquero joined Señor Mendez's party and after a few minutes, they left the camp together. However, ten minutes later, another party left the camp and with them, wrists lashed behind their back, were the Mexican workers from Pine Valley.

Fortunately, they appeared to be headed in the opposite direction to Señor Mendez's group. Luke correctly guessed these Mexicalaros were headed for a rendezvous with the Apaches.

As silently instructed by Drago, his lieutenant, Lomax, had made his way to the Grandes' wagon. Whilst all eyes were watching the departure of their leader Lomax reached the old wagon and peered into the back of it to check on the prisoners. It was the last thing he did, but it was Matt not Luke who dealt him the fatal blow.

During the Civil War, hand-to-hand fighting had become second nature to Matt. As a result, he was far less squeamish about using a knife than his cousin. As Lomax drew back the canvas covering the end of the wagon, Matt, knife in hand, moved silently out of the remuda and struck Lomax with it. So expert was Matt, that Drago's lieutenant was dead before he hit the ground.

Matt propped up the body against one of the wagon's good wheels so that to the casual observer it would seem that Lomax was taking his ease whilst guarding the wagon. Then, he climbed into it.

The sight inside lived long in his memory: tilted at a crazy angle, the floor of the wagon was still half full of whiskey crates. Mr and Mrs Grande were lashed to a pile of them; their feet and hands were tied together, making it almost impossible for either of them to move. Elizabeth was not only tied to another crate, but she was gagged. Laura had been treated in the same manner although tied to a different crate yet her gag proved to be a blessing in disguise, since it prevented her from crying out in surprise at the sight of Matt.

Using his blood-stained knife, Matt cut the Grandes' bonds. While they were quietly restoring their circulation, he released Elizabeth. She smiled, but realizing the need for silence, said nothing.

Matt was afraid that Laura would not be so sensible and her cries of joy at being released might raise the alarm. But he underestimated her for she said nothing. How could she? Her first action was to fling her arms tightly round Matt him and kiss him passionately.

Unfortunately for Matt, the escape plan required that he kept to the strict timetable devised by Luke, so reluctantly, he disentangled himself from Laura's embrace and gave the six-gun he had taken from Lomax to Mr Grande.

While he did so, Luke sought to find Josh in the remuda. Although the rest of the horses had been hobbled, the great black stallion had been tethered to a young cottonwood. As a result, the rest of the remuda were between Josh and the camp, making Luke's task easier than he had dared hope.

Better still, the great stallion had not yet been unsaddled. This was not so surprising, since Josh had so far unseated everyone unwise enough to try to ride him. After that, none of the Mexicalaros had been prepared to go near the stallion's flashing hoofs.

Next to Josh was a fine looking mustang and it too was still saddled. This was because Drago always kept one reliable horse at the ready so that he could escape in the unlikely event of the camp being attacked by overwhelming odds.

114

Luke led it and Josh as quietly as possible through the cottonwoods and away from the camp. Only when he was certain that he was safe from discovery did he mount Josh and, leading the mustang, ride away. After an hour, he reached a large outcrop of rocks, where he dismounted. He was greeted by a chorus of whinnies from Spike and the other horses they had left hidden behind the outcrop.

Safe in the knowledge that the rest of the Mexicalaros mistakenly thought that Lomax had fallen asleep in front of the wagon, Matt waited for sundown. By that time most of the Mexicalaros were well on the way to getting drunk. Carefully, Matt sliced through the wagon's canvas side with his still blood-stained knife. Of course, he chose the side opposite the main camp, facing the remuda.

Led by Matt, one by one the prisoners climbed down from the wagon. Using the wagon and the piles of saddles as cover, he led them behind the remuda. As soon as it was completely dark, they made their way through the cottonwoods and into the dry gulley along which he, Luke and the vaquero had approached the camp.

The moon had not yet risen, so there was no need to crawl. But in the gloom, their progress was slow and it was almost twenty minutes before Matt deemed they were far enough away from the camp to talk. Even then, he insisted they spoke in whispers.

They had not much to tell that Matt had not already pieced together. Laura remained silent but grasped Matt's hand firmly and refused to let go. But they had to push on and the difficult going brought an end to the talking. With Laura by his side, Matt led, Elizabeth followed and Mr and Mrs Grande brought up the rear.

All too soon, the moon, a full one, began to rise. If its light helped them on their way, it also made them plainly visible. There was now absolutely no cover and what may have been a short ride for Luke was a relatively long walk for them.

Matt tried not to show the anxiety he felt. On foot and armed with only two six-guns and his knife, they would stand little chance out in the open. With the moonlight to aid them, the Mexicalaros would have little difficulty in picking up the prints of the women's shoes as their heels dug into the ground, still soft after the rain storm.

However, in spite of Matt's fears, they reached the outcrop of rocks without incident. Luke leapt down and embraced his wife with all the passion of a newly wed. Exhausted, Mr and Mrs Grande sank to the ground, while Laura remained glued to Matt's side.

They were all tired. Nevertheless, they could not rest for long. Desolation Ford was the only safe place to cross the Rio Grande, so to have any chance of escaping, they had to get to it before the Mexicalaros. Matt's main hope was that the outlaws would drink themselves into a stupor causing them to oversleep in the morning.

But even after they had crossed the Rio Grande, they would still not be safe. The JT ranch house was many miles away from the river and with only five horses between the six of them, one horse would have to carry two people. Even if the extra load was shared between the horses, they would still have to be rested often.

Luke, with Elizabeth sitting behind him, took the lead. Josh seemed not to notice the extra weight. Mrs Grande managed quite well but Laura, unused to riding, found the task was beyond her. So Elizabeth took her steed and Laura sat behind Matt clinging to him tightly. If Spike was in any way troubled by his double load he was not about to show it: whatever Josh had done, he would match.

Although it was far from an unpleasant sensation, it seemed to Matt that Laura clung to him a little tighter than was absolutely necessary.

117

However, he put it down to the terrible ordeal she had been through rather than any romantic inclinations on her part.

CHAPTER ELEVEN

Dawn found them in sight of Desolation Ford. At this point, the well-worn trail offered little cover. However, that was not their main concern, for in front of them was a ghastly and gruesome sight: from the bough of a huge tree hung the bodies of Señor Mendez and his vaqueros. It appeared they had been shot, but not fatally. Even though they had been badly wounded, Drago and his men had then strung them up and left them to die in agony.

Horrified, they dismounted.

'What sort of men could do such a terrible thing?' asked Laura.

'They aren't men, they're beasts, far worse than the Apaches,' said Mr Grande grimly.

'We can't just leave them hanging like that,' said Elizabeth biting back her tears.

'I'm afraid we must,' said Matt. 'If we cut them down, the Mexicalaros will know we've been here.'

'If they return, they will pick up our trail, anyway,' said Luke. 'But we haven't the tools to give them a decent burial even if we had the time.'

'Agreed, although the horses will have to be rested soon,' said Matt.

'But not on this side of the Rio Grande. We must get across the ford at once or we may all finish up like Señor Mendez and his men,' said Luke grimly.

With Laura clinging precariously behind him, Matt drove Spike into Desolation Ford and the rest followed. Progress was slow; Elizabeth and Mrs Grande needed all the help their respective husbands could give and all the time they were crossing the Rio Grande, they made easy targets. But still there was no sign of the Mexicalaros so although they were soaked to the skin, they completed the crossing without incident.

They pushed on hard for about half an hour and then rested. Spike was almost exhausted but immensely proud: he had carried a double load twice as far as Josh.

While they were all resting, Luke had time to think about their situation. What had happened to Mr Thompson and his men? Señor Mendez was supposed to have led Drago and his men into a canyon Luke had found during his scouting trip. There, Mr Thompson and his men should have been waiting under cover, ready to pounce and take Drago and his Mexicalaros by surprise.

But it seemed that Señor Mendez had made for Desolation Ford and not the canyon. But why? What had happened to Mr Thompson and his men? Had they also been captured? Finally, why had Drago murdered Señor Mendez and his vaqueros?

So many questions, so few answers. A feeling of guilt spread over Luke. It had been his plan and he felt responsible for the appalling fate of Señor Mendez and his vaqueros. However, the feeling of guilt soon gave way to an ice cold anger. Dead or alive, proclaimed all the Wanted posters he still had on Drago. In spite of his elaborate precautions to bury his past, in that moment, Luke became a bounty hunter again: Drago would not go unpunished.

But that was for the future. So when the horses had been rested, they moved on. This time Laura sat on Josh behind Luke and Mrs Grande noticed she did not cling as tightly to him as she had done to Matt.

They headed for the old adobe cabin, but although they spent much of the time dreading pursuit, they reached it without incident. How much longer could their luck last, Matt wondered?

While the men tended the horses, the women lit the kitchen fire and began to cook a hot meal. Although it was only bacon and beans, it was the first hot meal the former prisoners had eaten for days and so it seemed like a feast.

Tired as he was, Matt elected to take first watch. The others bedded down and were all asleep in minutes. But an hour later, when all was quiet, Laura made her way over to Matt and much to his surprise, snuggled into him. Nothing was said for several minutes until she wrapped her arms around his shoulders and kissed him. But he quickly disentangled himself from her embrace.

'Enough. I'm supposed to be on watch,' he gasped apologetically.

'But I wouldn't be here to guard if you had not come to rescue me,' she said.

'Not just me. Don't forget Luke, it was his plan.' Matt thought it better not to remind Laura about Señor Mendez and his vaqueros.

'But he had Elizabeth to think about and, of course Mr and Mrs Grande. But you hardly know any of us!'

'Funny, I didn't think you were the type of girl to kiss a man she hardly knew, especially in the middle of the night.'

'Matt Connelly, what are you implying?' Laura blushed furiously.

'Shush! You'll wake the others.'

Laura froze as Mrs Grande stirred, but she soon settled down and Laura, although horribly embarrassed by her actions, spoke instinctively from her heart.

'I know enough about you to care about you,' she whispered.

'And I care for you. But I'm just a dollar-a-day cowboy. What sort of life could I give you?'

'Unless you give me the chance, how will I ever find out?'

He had no answer to her logic, so changed the subject.

'Time to speak about *our* future when we have destroyed the Mexicalaros,' he said gently.

For the first time Matt had said, *our* future. The words sent a tingle of excitement up and down her spine. But there was still one major obstacle to whatever future they might have:

'Matt, why do we have to go on fighting the Mexicalaros? We're safe now, aren't we?'

He thought for a moment before replying, then decided that Laura had a right to know the truth.

'I'm afraid not. The main weapon of the

Mexicalaros is fear. If it becomes known that a few men rescued the prisoners they were guarding and then got clean away, their reputation would be destroyed. So they must come after us and destroy us as an example to others. As long as we stay west of the Pecos, we must fight.'

'Is the West always this violent?' she asked in a shocked voice.

'Many parts of it are and may be for some years to come. But if enough good people get together and fight for what is right, law and order will win out, one day.'

'Matt, Texas is so different from my home, but I don't suppose you would like to live back east in Boston?' she asked as pointedly as she dared.

'Laura, ranching and the wide open spaces of the West is all I know. I'd be like a fish out of water in any large city.'

For some minutes they sat in silence. Laura mulled things over. Of course, Matt was right. Boston was a long established and sophisticated city. It had proper streets and fine houses and its people had long used lawyers rather than six-guns to settle their differences. She couldn't expect him to live there.

Matt was also thinking about Boston. It was Laura's home and he imagined her married to a lawyer or a banker and living in some luxurious mansion with many servants. What right had he to ask her to marry him and settle down in the dangerous wilderness of the Texas panhandle? None, came the instant reply from his conscience.

Laura's continued silence only served to confirm Matt's belief. But once again he was wrong, she was simply enjoying the security of his arm about her and desperately trying to stay awake.

But exhaustion won, so determined not to make more of a fool of herself than she already had, she returned to her bunk. She was asleep in seconds, but there was only room in her dreams for the cowboy who had risked his life to rescue her.

After another couple of hours or so, Luke awoke. After reluctantly untangling himself from the arms of his wife, he took over the watch from his cousin. Matt climbed into a spare bunk and was also asleep in an instant. Yet his dreams were all dark and not about Laura.

All through the rest of that long night, Luke kept watch. Concerned over how much the ordeal had taken out of his father-in-law, he let Mr Grande sleep until just before dawn. Then, with even greater viligance they kept watch together. However, as dawn broke, there was no sign of the Mexicalaros.

As the women slept on, Matt awoke. Then, in hushed voices, a council of war took place. Their first concern was Matt's boss, John Thompson. What had happened to him and his men? Had they too fallen foul of Drago and his Mexicalaros? Their attention then turned to their own plight.

'With only five horses between us we would have no chance if the Mexicalaros caught us out in the open,' said Luke, 'so I think it's too dangerous to ride during daylight hours.'

'So what do you suggest?' asked Mr Grande.

'We stay here today and start out for the JT ranch tomorrow evening.'

'But what if the Mexicalaros catch us here?' asked Mr Grande.

'With only one repeating rifle between us, Matt and I made a successful stand in this cabin against at least a dozen Mexicalaros. Now there are three of us and we each have a Winchester plus those we left here.'

'What about food and water?' asked Mr Grande.

'There's a large barrel full of water in the kitchen,' said Matt. 'Although we have used up all the bacon, I guess there is enough food to last a couple of days. That's providing nobody minds living on beans and sourdough.'

'In that case Matt, if you don't mind keeping

126

watch again, I'll go hunting,' said Luke.

'And I'll tend the horses. They all need feeding and rubbing down, even if there isn't time to groom them properly,' said Mr Grande.

The sound of shots woke up the women.

'Have the Mexicalaros found us?' asked Laura anxiously.

'No,' laughed Matt. 'It's just Luke catching our next meal.'

CHAPTER TWELVE

The next day, one hour after dawn, the Mexicalaros attacked. At least thirty of them galloped in one great charge towards the old adobe line cabin. Clearly Drago had delayed the attack until he had received reinforcements.

However, those inside the line cabin were well prepared. The concentrated fire from three Winchesters ripped into the charging riders. Man after man fell, yet the rest of the Mexicalaros still advanced at full gallop.

But there was no respite for them. As soon as Matt had emptied his Winchester, Laura passed him a fully loaded one. Elizabeth did the same for Luke and Mrs Grande acted as loader for her husband. In that way they were able to maintain a continuous barrage. But not without cost: an unlucky shot ricocheted off the window shutter and struck Mr Grande in his right shoulder.

He could no longer fire his Winchester, so as Mrs Grande tended the wound, Laura moved to the vacated window, picked up the Winchester and started to shoot. It's doubtful if she actually hit anyone, unless it was a lucky shot, since she had never fired any sort of gun in her life. But at least the volume of fire was kept up and it continued to be so as Elizabeth moved between the shooters reloading their discarded empty carbines.

The assault lasted about twenty minutes before Drago called it off. His men retreated beyond the range of the Winchester carbines, but not beyond the range of the Henry rifles the Mexicalaros had taken from Pine Valley.

Now the tables were turned and with a vengance: those in the line cabin were pinned down by fire they could not return. Although the Mexicalaros had lost many men in their wild cavalry charge, there were still enough of them left to surround the line cabin, and unlike the leader of the first attack on the cabin, Drago had infinite patience. The siege would last until the cabin was taken, its occupants killed and the Winchesters inside it were his.

Inside the line cabin the mood was sombre as

the incumbents assessed their chances.

'Is there any hope of rescue?' asked Laura anxiously.

Matt thought hard. Again he decided that an honest appraisal of their situation was the best policy.

'Very little,' he replied. 'Even if Paulo brings back reinforcements, there's no telling if he will be able to bring enough men back to make any difference.'

'But we must do everying we can to hold out as long as possible,' said the wounded Mr Grande.

'Sit still while I tend your wound, darling,' admonished Mrs Grande.

Luke, who had been silent throughout their deliberations, went to guard the front door. Elizabeth picked up another Winchester and then stood watch out of the side window.

Matt went into the kitchen to examine Mr Grande's wound. Laura followed him and tended the fire; fortunately there was ample provision of firewood, so they would not have to go without coffee or hot food.

In spite of his wife's care, Mr Grande had lost a considerable amount of blood, but the wound was not too serious. Fortunately, the bullet had been almost spent by the time it struck but nevertheless,

Matt knew it had to be removed as soon as possible. During the war, he had seen too many of his fellow soldiers die from lead poisoning to doubt that.

'I'll need boiling water and something clean to bind up the wound,' he said to Mrs Grande.

Laura overheard Matt. While her aunt was boiling the water, she calmly removed her cotton blouse. Then, quite deliberately, tore off both sleeves and gave them to Matt. It was not until she was quite sure he had enough material to swab out the wound and fashion a suitable bandage that she put what was left of her blouse back on.

Matt had removed several bullets from wounded men during the war and this one was simpler than most, but with nothing to deaden the pain, Mr Grande's ordeal was still excruciatingly painful. However he remained conscious and calm throughout the operation.

There then began a stand-off between the besiegers and the besieged. Even taking into account Mr Grande's wounds, those within the cabin still had enough firepower to withstand almost any direct assault. But it would have been little short of suicide to attempt to reach the horses so the occupants of the line cabin were going nowhere.

The long day turned into an even longer night, but the Mexicalaros made no move. Clearly Drago's strategy was to starve out the occupants of the old line cabin. Whether this policy would have succeeded will never be known for the next day, the besiegers suddenly found themselves under attack from every quarter.

Intent on taking the cabin, Drago had neglected to post lookouts to protect the rear of his troops. Seemingly from out of nowhere, a deadly fusillade shattered the peace. It came from behind the Mexicalaros at the rear of the cabin. Several of them were hit; the survivors wheeled round to face their new assailants thus exposing their flank to Matt's deadly fire.

Before the Mexicalaros laying siege at the front of the cabin could retaliate they also found themselves under fire, again from behind. This time, there was only a single volley but it came from a dozen musket-rifles: it cut down five Mexicalaros.

Luke's Winchester then added to the general devastation. Its deadly fire proved to be the last straw for the Mexicalaros. Caught beween the fire from the cabin and a new enemy that seemed to be all around them, the Mexicalaros at the front of the cabin turned and fled towards their horses.

Seeing them flee, the rest deserted their posts and followed suit.

But yet another force lay between the fleeing Mexicalaros and their horses. It consisted of six heavily armed vaqueros standing shoulder to shoulder, Springfields primed and ready to fire. Where they had come from and how they had reached the horses unobserved, the Mexicalaros never knew.

At point blank range, the vaqueros opened fire: all six of them hit their targets. Then, they threw down their musket rifles, drew their six-guns and as the Mexicalaros came into range, opened fire. But hitting a moving target with a six-gun requires a great deal of practice, especially when that target is shooting back.

The vaqueros were soon overrun, but neither the rest of their colleagues nor those in the cabin could fire at the Mexicalaros for fear of hitting the vaqueros and half of them were struck down in the general mêlée that followed.

Yet barely half of the fleeing Mexicalaros reached their remuda. Those that did mounted their horses, however, blinded by panic, none of the survivors noticed that all the cinches of the saddles had been loosened, so one by one, the Mexicalaros crashed to the ground. Three managed to remount their horses and, riding bareback, made good their escape. The rest, badly winded and utterly demoralized, surrendered.

So, in less than ten minutes, the much feared Mexicalaros had been routed. But by whom? At first, those within the cabin had no idea, but then they were hailed by a familiar voice from behind the cabin. It was Paulo.

'It's all over. It's quite safe to come out,' he called.

CHAPTER THIRTEEN

While the women remained inside the cabin with Mr Grande, the surviving Mexicalaros were rounded up and tied hand and foot by the vaqueros. Matt didn't recognize any of them, but as Paulo led their snow white horses into the corral he realized they were from the El Chicote ranchero. But what were they doing so far away from home? His chores finished, Paulo began to explain.

'As you know, I escaped from the raid on the Pine Valley ranch and fled to my uncle's ranch and he then raised a general alarm. As a result, word of the raid spread far and wide, even as far as the home of Fernando, the boy you rescued at Twin Buttes.'

One of the vaqueros then took up the story.

'As many riders as could be spared were immediately dispatched from the El Chicote ranch. We crossed the Rio Grande and rode onto Pine Valley. But there, we only found the vaqueros left by Señor Mendez. So after resting for the night, we followed the route of Señor Matt to the JT ranch.'

'By that time I had already returned to the JT ranch,' continued Paulo, 'so next day, we rode to the old line cabin. Finding it empty, we stayed the night and rode to Desolation Ford and crossed the Rio Grande. I guess if we had stayed there we might have intercepted my uncle and prevented his death. But instead, we headed straight for the blind canyon intending to rendezvous with Mr Thompson and his men.'

Mr Thompson then took over the story.

'We were in serious trouble. The leader of the Mexicalaros never intended to go to the blind canyon with Señor Mendez because it was the place his Mexican workers were to be handed over to the Apaches.'

'So Drago knew he was being led into a trap and must have decided to turn the tables on Señor Mendez,' said Matt.

'The prisoners and their escort arrived at almost the same time as the Apaches,' continued Mr

Thompson. 'Together they made a too formidable force for us to tackle, even though we had Winchesters. Instead, we stayed hidden in the rocks at the back of the canyon while the exchange took place and both sides left soon after. We didn't follow them but remained behind in the canyon, trying to decide what to do next. But before we had come to any decision, Paulo and the vaqueros arrived.'

'We couldn't let the prisoners remain in the hands of the Apaches, so we decided to follow them,' said Paulo.

'Once we caught up with them, there was never any doubt of the outcome. The Apaches had little chance against our combined fire power,' said Mr Thompson.

Paulo again took up the story.

'After we freed the prisoners, we left some of our party to guide them back to safety while the rest of us made for the old line cabin. As we approached Desolation Ford, we found the bodies of my uncle and his vaqueros hanging from that tree.'

The memory was still very painful and Paulo was choked with emotion. The young wrangler could not continue, so Mr Thompson helped him out.

'We stopped long enough to give the bodies a

137

decent burial and then continued on to the cabin, but of course, we heard shooting long before we reached it. However, so intent were the Mexicalaros in capturing the old cabin, they didn't cover their flanks, which made it easy to sneak up on them. The rest you know.'

Explanations over, Matt began to look over the captured Mexicalaros. Amongst them were several men whom they had captured at the battle of Twin Buttes and then released into the wilderness – it seemed they had not learnt from that experience. However, there was no sign of Drago.

Matt went to thank the El Chicote vaqueros only to find they were intending to hang the surviving Mexicalaros.

'Not in Texas,' said Matt firmly. 'Even west of the Pecos, we cannot hang that many men without a legal trial.'

'Of course not, señor,' said one of the vaqueros in perfect English. 'If Mr Grande is fit enough to travel, we will wait one hour after you and your ladies have departed. Then, we will take the Mexicalaros back across the Rio Bravo del Norte or Rio Grande as you call it. Once we are back in Mexico, all save one of the murdering vermin shall receive the justice their actions have earned them.'

'All but one of the Mexicalaros?' asked Matt.

'The first to reveal the whereabouts of the Mexicalaros hideout will be set free,' replied the vaquero.

'Señor, you have already done much for us. But while you are interrogating the Mexicalaros, will you find out why they rustled our branded stock and kidnapped the Grandes?' asked Luke who had just joined them.

'Of course, señor. If you would like to join us?'

While the Mexicalaros were being interrogated, Matt sought out Laura.

'Are you all right?' he asked anxiously.

'Yes, is the fighting over?'

'No, only your part in it. I'll get Mr Thompson to arrange an escort to take you and the rest of the Grandes to the JT ranch. I guess that's the safest place until we can get you back East.'

'Matt Connelly, I'm not going anywhere until I know all the fighting is over and you are safe. But we must get Mr Grande back to some sort of civilization where he can rest and get the treatment he needs.'

Supported by his wife, Mr Grande had made his way out of the cabin just in time to overhear his niece.

'Laura, don't start fussing over me too. My wife and daughter are more than enough!'

'We Grande women must stick together,' replied Laura.

'Can you ride, sir?' asked Matt.

'Of course I damn well can. It's only a flesh wound!' snorted Mr Grande angrily.

'Language, Jeremiah,' said his wife sternly.

'Fine,' said Matt. 'Now the Mexicalaros have been dealt with, there are plenty of spare horses, but what about you, Laura?'

'Well, I've only ever ridden side-saddle and I couldn't manage that mustang when we were escaping, but I'll try again,' replied Laura.

'Well, we will select the most gentle mustang we have and with a little practice you will find a cowboy saddle easier to ride than a side-saddle. But only if you're dressed for it,' said Matt, looking pointedly at Laura's long skirt.'

Laura blushed deeply, too embarrassed to speak, but Mrs Grande answered for her.

'Laura, none of us is really dressed for riding, but unless you propose to walk to Mr Thompson's ranch, you will have to hitch up or slit your skirt. Better to lose some of your modesty than walk, however shocking that may seem to you.'

Once again Laura's reply took Matt by surprise.

'Well, I have already cut the sleeves of my blouse to make bandages, so if Matt will lend me his knife

140

again, I'll go back to the cabin and make the necessary alterations, if you will help me,' she said looking at Mrs Grande.

While they were making the alterations, Matt looked around for Luke but he was nowhere to be seen and neither was his horse, Josh. His wife, Elizabeth, was involved in an animated conversation with one of the El Chicote vaqueros. Matt joined them.

'Luke has gone after Drago. But that devil has two other Mexicalaros with him,' said Elizabeth, trying, but failing to get the fear out of her voice.

'But why?' asked Matt.

'It's a long story,' replied the English speaking vaquero. 'Under Drago's leadership, the Mexicalaros were stealing branded beef and selling them as their own in Mexico. I'm afraid, if the price was favourable enough, there are a few of my fellow countrymen who would buy such cattle without questioning their true ownership.'

'But that doesn't explain the attack on Pine Valley,' said Matt.

Elizabeth took up the story.

'It seems the man who was behind all our troubles in Redrock, Colonel Masters, had two brothers and one of them was Drago. When Drago's lieutenant discovered that someone called

Grande had bought the Pine Valley ranch, he decided to take over the ranch and take us back to Drago. Of course, my father-in-law was at the ranch so it wasn't too hard to convince him Luke was just a drifter passing through and, as we hoped, they left him behind.'

Matt knew his cousin's reputation too well to think that Luke had gone after Drago with the intention of bringing the outlaw to justice. No, Luke would seek a showdown. But Drago had at least two men with him; he could not let his cousin face them alone.

'I'll go after him,' he said grimly.

He found Spike and saddled up the stallion. But he needed his Winchester and ammunition which were in the cabin. He had just finished collecting them when Laura tried to interrupt him, but he was in no mood to be delayed, so after a brusque goodbye, he left the cabin and made his way to Spike.

But Laura was not so easy to dismiss. With the help of Mrs Grande, she had split the front and rear of her long skirt. As a result, she revealed as much of her shapely legs as any chorus-line girl as she hurried after him carrying a canteen full of water. Indeed, with her now sleeveless blouse also in tatters her appearance was far removed from the prim eastern girl Matt had first met at Luke's ranch barely two weeks ago.

Yet, if her lack of modesty bothered her, it didn't show. There was something else she had to show Matt.

'Elizabeth tells me you're also going after Drago and his men,' she said breathlessly.

'Yes, I can't let Luke face them alone, so please don't try and stop me.'

'Of course not, Matt. While Mr Thompson is arranging our escort back to his ranch, I just wanted to give you something to remember me by.'

With that, she threw herself into his arms and in front of all the vaqueros and their prisoners, kissed him passionately. But once again, circumstances forced Matt to disentangle himself from her embrace. Without another word, he mounted Spike and rode away; Laura watched until man and horse were out of sight.

CHAPTER FOURTEEN

The ground was still soft from the heavy rain, making the tracks of Luke's horse, Josh, easy to follow. Soon Matt reached a spot where they merged into those made by three more horses. As they led towards the Rio Grande it needed little skill to work out they had been made by the horses ridden by Drago and his men.

Nor did it take any skill in picking up their trail on the Mexican side of Desolation Ford – Drago and his men had made no attempt to conceal their horses' tracks. It seemed they were only interested in putting as much distance between themselves and the old line cabin as possible.

Yet their mustangs were no match for Josh. As

long as they left such a clear trail to follow, Matt had no doubt that Luke would overhaul them. But could Spike outrun Josh? He had to catch up with Luke before his cousin caught up with the outlaws: the chase was on.

The tracks veered away from the trail taken by the Grandes' old wagon and then headed due south, running west of the range of hills in which the Mexicalaros were rumoured to have their headquarters. The tracks remained easy to follow but after about two hours Matt reached a much wider and well worn trail.

So well used, Matt could no longer pick out the tracks left by Josh or the outlaws' horses. Should he turn east or head westwards? Matt's first instinct told him to take the east road for that trail seemed to wind back into the hills and therefore, towards the hideout of the Mexicalaros.

But there was no need to make an immediate decision for the gallant Spike needed rest. Nearby, there was a small pool, filled to overflowing by the recent storm. Matt rode over to it, dismounted and allowed Spike to drink a little while he again pondered which direction to take.

Drago and his men must have realized they would be pursued. So, if the headquarters of the Mexicalaros had been their intended destination, surely they would have headed back to their camp and then continued past the old wagon into the hills. That would have been a much shorter route to their secret headquarters.

So that could not be their destination and, when Spike was rested, Matt took the westward trail. He rode until nightfall and then unsaddled Spike and hobbled the stallion using his rope. All cowboys carried one but it was usually referred to by easterners as a lasso. Next, he lit a small fire and ate half the provisions Laura had packed for him.

Spike had covered the ground superbly. Even if the magnificent Josh had outpaced him, the mustangs of Drago and his men could not have done so. Therefore, confident he had significantly narrowed the gap between himself and the outlaws, he settled down and, using his saddle as a pillow, was asleep in seconds.

Matt rose early, ate the last of his provisions and just as dawn was breaking, set off in pursuit of his cousin. All morning, he followed the well used trail and yet saw nobody.

A little before noon, the track led to a small and apparently unnamed settlement which comprised a very large and imposing livery stable but then nothing more than a few adobe houses, a general store and a small cantina which doubled up at

146

night as a saloon.

As Matt rode slowly past the livery stable, he noticed several fine horses and many more mustangs, all being attended to by about a dozen Mexicans. Indeed, the size of the livery stable seemed totally out of proportion to the small settlement it served.

He needed provisions so, despite a feeling of unease which he could not explain, he dismounted and went into the general store. To his surprise, the Mexican serving in the store spoke perfect English.

'Where can I get a decent meal?' he asked.

'In the cantina, señor, they are quite used to serving Americans.'

As Matt slowly walked across the street, he began to piece the jigsaw together. It wasn't the horses from the settlement the livery stable catered for, it was for the mustangs of Mexicalaros, hence its size.

There had been several Americans in the outlaw band, so to get their business at least some of the locals spoke English. And that meant the American Mexicalaros must have spent a lot of time in the settlement.

The answer hit him with the force of a steam hammer: the Mexicalaros' secret base was not in the border hills as had been generally supposed, it

147

was here in this settlement. And that was why Drago and his two men had ridden here. They were probably waiting for him in the cantina at this very moment. It was too late to turn back, if he was right – to do so would surely invite a bullet in the back.

For extra speed, his six-gun had a hairpin trigger so, to prevent any chance of an accidental firing, he kept its first chamber empty. But not today. As he reached the sidewalk, he paused to reload the empty cylinder: his gut instinct told him he was going to need it.

The inside of the cantina was gloomy, especially in the far corner. There, a solitary man in a poncho slouched over his table, a big Mexican sombrero tipped drunkenly over his face.

Otherwise, there were only a few Mexicans drinking at the far end of the American style long bar. There appeared to be little danger, yet his instinct told him that something was wrong. He was sure he had walked into a trap, although he could not see what it was.

'What can I get you, señor?' asked the Mexican barman. He too spoke in perfect English.

'Tequila,' said Matt bruskly.

As the barman served him, Matt gave no sign he was aware of any danger. But his eyes never left the long mirror above the bar. From their tenseness, it seemed the Mexicans at the far end of the bar were also waiting for something to happen.

'You are far from home,' said the barman pleasantly.

'Not really. Since the war, my home is where I hang my hat.'

'Yet your nose sticks ever into my business.'

It was Drago. Whilst Matt had been watching the Mexicans at the other end of the bar through the mirror, the outlaw had entered the cantina through a side door and behind him were his two henchmen. The trap had been sprung.

Matt was outgunned. If he turned to face Drago and his two Mexican henchmen, he would have to turn his back on the other Mexicans at the other end of the bar: he was trapped. Evidently Drago thought so too, for instead of pressing home his advantage, he started to gloat.

'Do you think me a fool? We have been aware you have been following us since we left that accursed cabin. What do you think you could achieve on your own?'

'Not on his own, Drago. And I've been after you for long before you attacked the line cabin.'

With a crash, the man who had been slouched over the table stood up and kicked away his chair.

149

Then he pulled his poncho to one side to reveal a Remington six-gun.

'Whoever you are, stay out of my business,' snarled Drago.

'My name is Luke Donovan, and catching you, dead or alive, is my business.'

Clearly Drago had already heard of the name as Matt saw fear in his eyes as he turned and drew. In the same instant Matt also reached for his six-gun, yet his target was not Drago but his two henchmen. As they drew against him, Matt saw the barman reach under the bar, where all of his ilk usually kept a shotgun.

Drago was quick, but Luke was quicker. His bullet thudded into the outlaw's chest just as Drago's six-gun cleared its holster. Drago was dead before his finger could tighten on his trigger and the gun fell out of his hand.

If Matt could not quite match the speed of the two professional gunmen, he was no slouch and was too fast for Drago's henchmen. The impact of his bullets, at such close range, blew them off their feet and sent them crashing into a table, knocking it over as they fell.

But Matt had no time to watch them: in one smooth motion he swivelled towards the bar and fired. The barman had already turned to aim at

Luke but Matt's bullet struck him in the side of his shoulder, knocking him off balance, just as he fired both barrels.

As Luke whirled to face the other Mexicans, the buckshot, which could have gone anywhere, hit the Mexicans at point blank range. Matt had seen and heard many terrible things during the war, but nothing to compare with the effect of this buckshot – it literally tore the Mexicans to pieces, yet did not kill them instantly: their dying screams of agony as their life blood gushed out on to the cantina's floor, remained with Matt for the rest of his life.

'Cousin, help me get Drago's body out of here,' Luke said urgently.

Matt was too stunned to argue. Together they carried the body of Drago over the bodies of his two henchmen, out of the cantina and draped it unceremoniously over his horse.

While Matt tied Drago's body to the saddle of his horse, Luke went round to the back of the cantina to where he had hitched Josh. If they were to get out of the settlement unharmed, time was of the essence. Even so, a small crowd had begun to gather before he and Matt were ready to ride away.

Fortunately, the small crowd was either too stunned or too frightened to offer any resistance so Matt and Luke were able to ride away quite safely. Nevertheless they galloped hard for as long as Drago's mustang could manage. Of course, Josh could have gone on much longer and if Spike felt the pace after his hard morning ride, he wasn't about to show it in front of Josh.

'Why do we need Drago's body?' asked Matt when they rested the horses.

'We need his body to claim the reward. Since I'm supposed to be dead, that has to be your job. But it will be worth the effort – according to my old Wanted posters, the reward should be at least fifteen hundred dollars,' said Luke.

On their way back to Desolation Ford, they met the vaqueros from El Chicote. They had disposed of the Mexicalaros, so had decided to follow Matt and Luke to help to catch Drago.

They were delighted to see the outlaw was dead, but they also had a grisly tale to tell. They had just shepherded the Mexicalaros prisoners across Desolation Ford when they were intercepted by a large Apache war party. But it was the Mexicalaros they wanted, not the El Chicote vaqueros – they blamed the prisoners for the attack on their fellow braves who had been escorting Mr Grande's workers.

The Apaches were thirsting for revenge and the

vaqueros had been in no mood to risk their lives to protect Mexicalaros so they agreed to the demands of the Apaches in return for safe conduct out of their territory.

Prolonged torture before a long, agonizing death was the probable fate of the Mexicalaros. How ironic, thought Matt, after the many terrible atrocities they had committed, the Mexicalaros should die for an attack for which they not responsible.

EPILOGUE

There were few towns west of the Pecos from which the reward money could be claimed, but Cottonfields was one and in his days as a bounty hunter, Luke had several times cut a deal with its sheriff. For that reason, it was Matt and not Luke that made his way to the little town.

However, it was several days' ride away and haste was necessary for Drago's body needed official identification before it could be buried. Once again Spike was up to the task but Drago's mustang was near to exhaustion by the time they reached Cottonfields.

Although he did cut a deal, the sheriff of Cottonfields was an honest man. For ten per cent of the reward money, the sheriff gave the necessary identification, had the body buried and sent all the necessary paperwork back east via the weekly stage. Even so, collecting the reward money took much longer than Matt expected and it was some weeks before he was able to return to the JT ranch. As he expected, the Grandes had only stayed there a few days after Luke had arrived before returning to Pine Valley.

During Matt's absence, the JT cowhands had returned from Dodge. The herd had been sold at a handsome price; there was more than enough money for Mr Thompson to redeem in full the ranch's mortgage, pay off all the other outstanding debts and renovate the ranch house. And after all that, there would still be sufficient money to finance the running of the ranch for a whole year, until the next herd was sold.

As a result, there had been an amazing transformation. New hands had been hired, although Mr Thompson had sent most of them to the Pine Valley ranch to help in the cattle round up. If Luke's ranch was to prosper, cattle had to be branded and fattened up before undertaking the long trek north to be sold at one of the railhead towns such as Abilene or Dodge.

The JT ranch house had already been repainted. Anything deemed beyond repair had been torn down and was either in the process of being rebuilt or already had been.

Matt stayed only long enough to allow Spike to rest before heading for Pine Valley. The reward for Drago had risen since Luke had given up bounty hunting and even after the sheriff of Cottonfields had taken his cut there was almost eighteen hundred dollars reward money in his saddle-bags. However, he felt most of it belonged to Luke.

The Pine Valley ranch was also a hive of activity. Most of the Mexicans rescued by Mr Thompson were busy making good the damage done by the Mexicalaros. Elizabeth came out to greet Matt and confirmed that the Grandes had left for their own ranch near Redrock. Matt naturally assumed that Laura had gone with them.

Luke was out on the range supposedly leading the JT hands on the round up. But truth to tell, he was learning what to do rather than instructing. Elizabeth sent Paulo to fetch him.

'Matt, what am I thinking, keeping you outside?' she said. 'Do come in and wash up. Breakfast will be ready by the time you've finished. *We* have been expecting you.'

Matt returned from his ablutions to find that Luke had come back and was already sitting at the breakfast table. Elizabeth sat beside him but did not stay for breakfast.

It was a splendid meal, but who had cooked it? Sadly, the Chinese cook had been killed during their raid on the ranch, but with Drago and his band of desperados destroyed, the Mexicalaros would never again terrorize the land west of the Pecos.

Over breakfast, the reward money was discussed.

'Half is yours, you earned it,' insisted Luke.

'But you outdrew Drago, so you ought to get the lion's share. Besides, you have Elizabeth to think of and. . . .'

Matt broke off in mid sentence as Laura, dressed in her finest clothes, entered the dining room. She had been preparing breakfast when Matt arrived but had not wanted him to see her dressed in her old kitchen attire so she stayed in the kitchen until she had finished cooking. Then, while Matt and Luke were eating breakfast and discussing the reward money, she hurried to her bedroom and while she changed into her best dress, Elizabeth brushed her hair.

It took some time but eventually she was satisfied with her appearance and, with Elizabeth by her side, made her dramatic entrance.

The effect on Matt was all she had hoped: taken completely by surprise, he rose hastily and barely managed to stammer a welcome.

157

'I thought you had gone back east,' he said at last.

During his absence, Laura had rehearsed this meeting many times in her mind and it had seemed so easy. Yet now it was really happening, she felt her courage ebb away so she took a deep breath and answered Matt.

'I may still do so, unless you give me a reason to stay,' she said as pointedly and as brazenly as she dared.

Elizabeth had followed Laura into the dining room and she interrupted before the still startled Matt could respond.

'Come Luke, I need your help in the kitchen.'

Obediently Luke left. Matt tried to use the brief time until they were alone to think out an answer to Laura's questions but the same old doubts clouded his judgement.

'Of course I want you to stay, but what sort of life can a dollar-a-day cowhand offer a city bred girl like you?'

She didn't answer. Instead, she was in his arms in a flash. They were still locked in a deep embrace when Elizabeth returned interrupting them.

'Luke tells me that you have not accepted your share of the reward money,' she said.

'No,' agreed Matt.

'So why not use it to buy into the Pine Valley ranch? Then we could build an extension for you and Laura. No offence intended, Matt, but aren't you getting a bit too old to be a cowboy?' asked Elizabeth pertly.

'But would Luke agree?'

'Of course. We've all ready discussed it, haven't we, Laura? We thought a quarter share would be fair. That would make you a fully fledged ranch owner and Laura a rancher's wife.'

'It seems you women have already decided,' said a bewildered Matt.

'You bet they have and I for one know better than to argue against their schemes,' laughed Luke as he returned.

'But I haven't asked Laura to marry me,' protested Matt.

'But you will, won't you, darling?' said Laura, smiling contentedly.